"No, Nic

"You're wrong about that. It's one of the best I've come up with in a long time."

Nick started to lower his mouth to hers again. Ryleigh backed out of his arms, pushing wisps of hair off her forehead with a shaky hand. "We have rules—"

"Screw the rules."

"We talked about this. We set them up for a reason." Clouds slid into her eyes as the passion faded and doubt took its place. "As much as I'd like to keep this up, I don't want to lose you as a friend. If we go down this path, I'm afraid that's what would happen."

"It won't. I promise."

Ryleigh's smile was bittersweet. "I know you mean that. You're the most honorable man I've ever met and you'd never deliberately break your word. But if we don't stick to the basics we established, you might not be able to keep that promise. And I'm not willing to take the chance…"

Dear Reader,

When I first started on my publication journey, the reality of seeing one of my books on a shelf in the store seemed beyond my reach. Day after day, I sat at the computer putting in precious time on a project with no guarantee of success, but the alternative was to never have tried. That was unacceptable.

I tapped into those feelings for the heroine in this book. Ryleigh Evans desperately wants to have a baby before turning thirty and she wants her ex-husband to be the father. Dr. Nick Damian is great with his pediatric patients but emotional baggage got in the way of being a good husband. He's not quite sure how his ex-wife talked him into helping with her dream, but somehow it becomes less about a baby and more about a second chance at love.

Thanks to all of you readers I'm still living my dream. I hope you enjoy reading this story as much as I enjoyed writing it.

All the Best!

Teresa Southwick

TO HAVE THE DOCTOR'S BABY

TERESA SOUTHWICK

SPECIAL EDITION

Recycling programs
for this product may
not exist in your area.

ISBN-13: 978-0-373-65608-0

TO HAVE THE DOCTOR'S BABY

TERESA SOUTHWICK

lives with her husband in Las Vegas, the city that reinvents itself every day. An avid fan of romance novels, she is delighted to be living out her dream of writing for Harlequin Books.

This book is dedicated to every woman with a dream.
Never give up!

Chapter One

They were the poster couple for an amicable divorce, but that didn't mean seeing her ex-husband on the first day of a new job wasn't nerve-racking.

Ryleigh Evans was about to test the boundaries of their comfortable friendship and knew it was an exam she could flunk spectacularly. Any minute he would arrive in her office and she was bracing for impact. Trying to, anyway.

At Mercy Medical Center, Nick Damian, M.D., was a legend. But how did one prepare to ask a legend for the biggest favor ever?

Blackmail would be good if she had something on him, but she didn't.

Opening the top button on her blouse and showing a little cleavage might help. The problem was she didn't have much in the way of cleavage and what she did have hadn't impressed him while they were married. Two years later there was no reason to believe that had changed. Against the odds, they now had a warm and supportive friendship that she didn't want to lose.

Ryleigh had just moved back to Las Vegas from Baltimore to take the position of regional coordinator for Children's Medical Charities. The organization raised money and funded kids' projects at the hospital. Nick was a pediatric pulmonologist and it was only a matter of time until their paths crossed. She just didn't want the crossing to be another *Titanic*. Hence this private meeting in her office, the first available time slot in their busy schedules since she'd returned.

There was a knock on her door that seemed as loud as a gunshot and just as startling. Even though she'd been expecting it.

"Too late for cleavage," she whispered before calling out, "Come in."

Her heart was pounding and she didn't actually hear the door open, but it must have because Nick was standing there. In worn jeans and a long-sleeved white cotton shirt, one wouldn't peg him as a doctor, but the stethoscope draped around his neck was a big clue. When not wearing scrubs, this was as professional as he dressed because he'd told her once that kids were intimidated by a suit. And a tie turned into a handy weapon for a pissed-off pediatric patient who'd been poked by needles one too many times and wanted to choke someone.

She stood, walked around her desk and stopped in front of him, then reached up to give him a hug. "Hi, Nick. It's really wonderful to see you."

His arms folded her close and felt warm, strong, familiar. A bittersweet feeling squeezed her heart, but she pushed it away. This wasn't about the past. She was working on her future.

"Ryleigh," he said, against her hair. "Welcome back."

When her heart started to race, she backed several steps away and asked, "How are you?"

"Fine. You?"

"Never better." Her voice was full of forced perkiness, which she hoped he didn't notice. It had been close to two years since they'd seen each other face-to-face. Their contact had been long phone calls, text messages and emails. They talked about everything including politics, books and movies. "You look great."

Understatement of the century.

He studied her with eyes that were an especially intense shade of blue and turned down just a little at the corners. They gave him a sad look, one that made every softhearted female and some who weren't so sensitive want to hug him and make whatever was bothering him better. She wasn't immune, and pushed that feeling away.

"Your hair is shorter," he finally said.

"Yeah."

Automatically she reached up and brushed her palm over the brunette layers that barely touched her shoulders. She was surprised he'd noticed. When they were married, she'd thought about shaving her head, to see if that would get his attention. But she was afraid he wouldn't even notice something that drastic and it could have destroyed her.

"I like it," he said.

"Thanks." The compliment started a glow inside her, but she refused to give it any traction. Back on task. "In case you're wondering why I asked for this meeting—"

"You figured it would be more private than bumping into me in the hospital cafeteria."

"Yes."

"And here we are. Being more private." He folded his arms over his chest and smiled as if he were a proud mentor. "Look at you. The new regional coordinator for CMC."

"How about that? I wanted to come back—for this job," she clarified. There was another agenda, but she needed to wait to spring that on him.

"Because of the kids," he guessed.

"That's one of the reasons."

"How long has it been? Two years?"

"That sounds about right. Since the divorce," she qualified.

"Longer then, since you moved to Baltimore before that."

"Yeah. I thought you'd come after me." Did she really say that out loud? She hadn't meant to. Something about seeing him deactivated the filter between her brain and mouth.

How naive she'd been then. She hadn't handled things well and took responsibility for the immature behavior. Her only excuse was that she'd been young and hopelessly in love. It had been almost a physical ache when she wasn't with him, which was pretty often since he always went when a patient called. He dropped everything, even her. She hadn't known how to ask for what she wanted then. But she was older, wiser and wouldn't make the same mistake now.

"Ry, if there was—"

"Ancient history," she interrupted. It didn't hurt anymore because she'd made herself fall out of love with him.

Nick was the only one who'd ever called her Ry and the familiarity combined with his regretful expression caught her off guard. It struck a chord inside her that hadn't been plucked since the last time she'd seen him, and the vibration was uncomfortable.

She backed away again, then turned and moved behind her desk to sit in the high-backed black chair. "The thing is, Nick, I'm back. And it's important to me to make sure you and I are okay."

"If we weren't, it would have been pretty easy to ignore your emails, texts and phone calls."

"Still. There's no facial expression with electronic communication."

"Meaning you can tell if I'm lying?" he teased.

"You would never lie." She believed that with every fiber of her being. "But *I* can see if you're okay."

"What you're getting at is whether or not I'm angry that you left. The answer is that I never was. I understood."

So not what she wanted to hear. If he'd said he hated her guts, she could live with that, proof of sorts that she'd been more important to him than a lamp shade. She wasn't proud of the fact that, on some level, leaving had been about getting an emotional reaction from him, just the tiniest clue that he'd cared even a little. She'd been looking for a sliver of hope that he could fit time in his schedule for her—for them.

She'd told him about the job offer on the East Coast and spun her own personal fantasy that he would pull out all the stops to talk her out of going. The truth was closer to him not even realizing she'd gone. None of that slipped out because it *was* ancient history. She'd moved on and had different aspirations.

But seeing him in the flesh reminded her why he was an important component of achieving her goal. He was just as handsome as the first time she'd seen him. His thick, dark hair with the waves barely slicked into submission still made her want to run her fingers through it. His cheeks and jaw were shadowed with scruff, just like she remembered. In the beginning of the separation, she'd actually missed the "beard burn" and wondered if she needed therapy.

He still looked good. Better than she remembered. Hotter than she'd hoped.

"We're fine, Ry," he said, meeting her gaze. "I was happy to hear you were the one hired for this job."

"You were?"

"Yeah. You'll be a good fit."

"Okay. I'm glad you think so." She smiled. One hurdle down. That cleared the way for the ultimate friendship test. "It's really wonderful to see you."

"Same here." The grin he flashed was hot enough to melt the polar ice cap.

Once upon a time it might have fed her fascination for him, but all this time away had worked magic. The dynamic between them was different. She could see him as an attractive man and not be sucked in by the charisma.

"I like this. Friendship is the new norm." Although she had other friends and none of them made her skin tingle with just a look. It would pass. "So, my friend, can we talk business?"

Nick rested a hip on the corner of her desk. "What kind of business?"

"Money," she said. "It's my job to raise it and I get to have a good deal of input on how to spend it."

"So, I need to be nice to you?" One of his dark eyebrows went up.

"It can't hurt." She was only half joking. Getting professional was a stall until she'd worked up the nerve to discuss what was really on her mind. "I'm meeting with all the doctors who specialize in pediatric medical disciplines to find out what the most pressing needs are. I'd like your wish list for how to use the money we raise."

Without hesitation he said, "ECMO."

"Would you care to translate for those of us who don't speak doctor?"

"Extra corporeal membrane oxygenation."

"That makes it much clearer," she said dryly. "Is it a machine or a process?"

"Both." Intensity shone in his eyes. "It works on the same principle as a heart-lung machine for babies with IRDS." When he saw her look, he added, "Infant respiratory distress syndrome."

"I need more information."

He thought for several moments, probably figuring out how to dumb it down for her. "When an infant's lungs get stiff, a respirator won't do the job. ECMO takes blood outside the body, channels it through a membrane to oxygenate it, then back in. This process is literally the difference between life and death."

"Then why doesn't the hospital have it now?" She had to ask even though she already suspected the answer.

"Cost prohibitive. The powers that be don't think it's a moneymaker."

Ryleigh knew that though the hospital was nonprofit, expenses still had to be met, revenue recovered through insurance payments and invoice collection, which was all channeled back into the facility. "What happens to the babies at risk now?"

"They get transferred to Phoenix or St. George, Utah. They're the closest hospitals that have the personnel and equipment. But getting them there takes a lot of time and that's the one thing these babies don't have."

"I see."

His gaze narrowed, a clue that he didn't believe she really got the severity of the need and was preparing to do battle. "ECMO is expensive."

"How much?"

"A million. Maybe more." He stood and put his palms flat on her desk, closing the space between them. "But the cost in terms of lives saved can't be calculated. Not only would kids here at Mercy Medical Center be helped, but other hospitals in the Vegas Valley could transfer critically ill babies here, too. In some cases adults could also be helped."

There was the intensity that had first captivated her, that passion to save lives she'd found so compelling. A passion she'd experienced on a personal level. A passion he carefully controlled. She'd eventually learned the sad lesson that professional dedication was a single-minded mistress and didn't share well with others.

"Look, Nick—"

"I know it's a long shot, Ry. But can you put a price tag on hope?"

How easily he'd slipped back into the familiar with her. That was both good and bad. "Get me the numbers."

"What?"

"I need to know what the actual cost is, and then we can talk."

He stared at her as if she had two heads. "Really?"

"Yes."

He grinned again. "Should have known you couldn't say no to a baby."

Baby.

One small word that tapped into her bottomless well of longing. She loved kids, all kids. The money this organization raised would go a long way to helping the sick ones get better, which was why she'd applied for this job. She'd taken it because more than anything she wanted a child of her own. This time around she and Nick were friends, and she knew how to ask for what she wanted.

Absently he picked up the nameplate from her desk and

looked at it and then her. "Ryleigh Evans. I didn't know you'd gone back to your maiden name."

"It wasn't information that I felt was text message worthy. Are you surprised?"

"Only that you haven't found a guy. Married. Started a family."

"It's not that easy." Not one man she'd dated had measured up to Nick. And he'd just given her the opening she was waiting for. "But you're right. I very much want to have a child."

"That was something we probably should have discussed before we got married."

By the time she'd brought up the subject, the marriage was already in trouble. Their relationship counselors agreed that bringing a baby into the mix would only accelerate the downward spiral.

"Yeah," she said. "But everything with us happened so fast."

She'd been so swept away by the dashing Dr. Damian. Nothing and no one could have convinced her that a man who fought so hard for a child's life wouldn't want children of his own. Then she'd brought up the subject.

She couldn't call that discussion an argument. Nick never argued. He was either called away for a patient or simply left. The last time he'd put her off, she did the leaving.

"It was my fault, Ryleigh. I just— It wasn't—" He shook his head in frustration—a doer, not a talker. "You'll find someone and get married, have children."

"One doesn't actually have to be married to have a baby. In all this time, I haven't met anyone who made me want to take the plunge again."

"It'll happen."

"What if it takes years and my eggs turn into raisins?

Advancing age and fertility are not compatible." She folded her hands and rested them on the desk. "My parents tried for years to have a baby and it didn't happen."

"Technically, that's not accurate because you're here."

"Yeah. But by the time they did, Mom was in her forties. She called me her miracle child." Dark memories came flooding back, losing first her father and a couple years later her mom. "Some miracle."

"It really was. Do you know the odds of a woman conceiving in her forties—"

"Please don't quote statistics. They were my parents and they died before I was out of high school. There was so little time with them, I used to wonder why they'd bothered. Now I understand the passion my mom felt, the yearning to have a baby because I feel it, too. But I also want to be young while my child is. More important, I want to actually be there while my child grows up."

"Don't sweat it. You're young—"

"Not that young." She stared at him. "I'm twenty-eight and a half. My biological clock is ticking and the prospects for marriage aren't looking good."

"Give it time," he said.

"I did that. And I'm finished holding my breath, Nick." The bar had been set really high and that was his fault. "I'm through with waiting."

"Do you have another choice?"

"As a matter of fact, I do. I can be a single mom."

"It's a big decision," he said.

"One I haven't come to lightly. I'm well aware of the difficulties. But I simply can't imagine my life without a child in it. I want to feel a baby grow and move inside me. More than anything, I want to hold my baby and raise him or her."

"But, Ryleigh, doing it alone—"

She held up a hand to stop him. "You're not going to talk me out of this."

"Someone has to make you see reason."

"Logic doesn't stand a chance against this longing to be a mother. Let me put it to you this way." She'd thought long and hard about what to say to him. "The need I have for a baby is as powerful as yours is for sex. Could you be talked out of it?"

"Point made." There was an uneasy expression on his face, a crack in the facade. "But how are you going to make it happen? In vitro? Potluck from a sperm bank?"

"I'd prefer not to do that." She met his gaze. "The hormone shots. The higher risk of it not being successful. Expense. Not to mention that the old-fashioned way is the first, best, most effective method."

"Then what?"

"Here's the thing, Nick. When we got married I was young and idealistic. All I needed to be happy was you, spending time with you. I'm older now and understand that you're a doctor and the kids need you. You're a gifted physician. You're also a good man, the best man I know. You have wonderful qualities and I've never met anyone more brilliant or dedicated. And it has to be said that you're not hard on the eyes."

"I hear a but."

"Only that I understand you couldn't give me what I needed. Not then, anyway."

"Here's the but," he said.

She nodded. "You can give me what I want now. And I want a baby."

When what she was asking for finally sank in, he looked like he'd swallowed his stethoscope. "That's a joke, right?"

"I've never been more serious."

"That's crazy." Nick stood and started to pace. "Do you realize what you're asking? A child would tie us together forever."

"It wouldn't have to."

He stopped and stared at her. "You expect me to father a child, then disappear?"

"We got married and you did that," she pointed out. "Not blaming you. Just saying… Look, I'm sorry to spring this on you, but there was really no good way to bring it up. And frankly, I'm glad it's out there. Take some time to think it over—"

"Done," he snapped. "And the answer is no."

"Just like that?"

"Yeah. You can't be serious. And when you come to your senses, we'll laugh about this."

Disappointment shuddered through her as hopes and dreams went on life support. "You know, when we were married, I actually thought about going off birth control. An 'accidental' pregnancy. An oops-the-condom-must-have-broken conversation."

"Why didn't you?" Surprise slid into his eyes as he stared down at her.

"It just wasn't right. I couldn't do it. Maybe this idea is insane, but at least it's straightforward and honest."

"I'm sorry, Ryleigh. I just can't go along with it."

"I had to ask." She worked hard at keeping the profound and emotional regret out of her voice. "I had a feeling you'd say no. So now it's on to plan B."

His gaze narrowed. "What's that?"

"I go to the second name on my list."

"That's not funny."

Bluffs never were. There was no list. This was about keeping her spunk factor in one piece. "I've never been more serious in my life."

* * *

Nick stood at the third-floor nurse's station in the PICU—Pediatric Intensive Care Unit—and finished charting. The job could be done sitting down, but he might fall asleep. After Ryleigh dropped the baby bombshell on him yesterday, getting to sleep last night had been a challenge he couldn't overcome. He was grateful for the emergency call that had kept him too busy to think. Fortunately the asthmatic kid was doing fine now. Him? Not so much.

He put the chart back, then walked down the hall and turned right toward the elevators. The familiar sound of Ryleigh's laughter drifted to him. At first he thought it was a hallucination due to sleep deprivation, until he saw her standing in front of the newborn nursery. There was a man with her. Carlton Gallagher. The doctor Nick was currently evaluating as a partner in his medical practice. The guy was smiling down at her. Was he the next name on her list?

The primal anger that blasted through Nick was shocking in its intensity.

Ryleigh had told him that she was completely serious about getting pregnant. It hadn't taken her long to move forward with plan B.

Nick's long stride quickly chewed up the length of the hall until he stopped beside them. "What's going on?"

He'd meant the question to be casual, but his tone had fallen far short of friendly to just this side of a hostile growl.

Ryleigh's puzzled expression was proof of that. "Hello, Nick. Dr. Gallagher just introduced himself. I'm glad you finally found someone to share the patient load in your practice."

"It's not a done deal," he said. "We're testing the water to see how we work together."

Carlton's gaze was challenging as he slid his hands into the pockets of his slacks. "A probationary period seemed wise, before we go to the trouble and expense of lawyers and contracts."

Nick had only evaluated this guy in a professional way. Gallagher had gone to one of the finest medical schools and graduated at the top of his class. He'd trained in Dallas at one of the best children's hospitals in the country and came highly recommended. After a couple months here at Mercy Medical he was getting high marks from the staff, too. Who were primarily of the female persuasion, so the poll results could be skewed.

The other doctor was about Nick's height, a little over six feet tall. His dark hair had some gray at the temples which probably made him look distinguished as opposed to old. Yeah, double standard. His eyes were brown. He was tan. And women would most likely think he wasn't bad looking. But was he brilliant? A good man? Not the best, because Ryleigh had first asked him, Nick, to father her baby. And the primal anger pushed through him again when his gaze dropped to Gallagher's naked left ring finger. His reaction must have showed because the other doctor tensed.

"It's getting late," he said. "I have to go."

Not exactly *gosh look at the time,* but close, and Nick felt a sense of satisfaction.

Ryleigh smiled up at him. "It was nice to meet you, Dr. Gallagher. And about the upcoming fundraiser, can I count on you to buy a table for the Children's Medical Charities Fundraiser Gala?"

"That's a question for the boss. Later, Nick." The other man met his gaze, frowned, then walked away.

Nick's work there was done and he started to say goodbye. Then he saw Ryleigh looking at the babies in isolettes in the newborn nursery on the other side of the glass. There were only a couple of infants since the majority of new mothers kept their babies in the room with them. Ryleigh would be one of those, judging by the tender yearning so plain on her face.

"So, are you settling in okay?" It was a lame question, but he didn't know what else to say. The favor she'd asked was like the elephant in the room, and he wanted out of there in the worst way. But he couldn't leave her looking like that. "Ryleigh?"

"You were kind of rude to Dr. Gallagher." She glanced over her shoulder at him. "Did you think I was hitting on your partner?"

"He's not my partner yet, and that wasn't rude. You know better than anyone that I have a limited capacity for people skills and it's reserved for the kids in peds."

"I thought about asking him to father my baby." There was teasing in her brown eyes when she turned and looked up at him. "But I decided that was a conversation better suited to a second meeting."

"Good idea." Not.

"Actually Spencer Stone crossed my mind," she said thoughtfully.

"My best friend?" A really bad idea just got worse.

"He's charming. Nice looking. A doctor, so he's smart." She was looking at the babies again. "Definitely on the list."

Nick hadn't believed she was serious about that. Now he wondered. "He's also shallow. Self-centered. And arrogant."

"I can live with that."

"Even though he breaks hearts on a regular basis?"

"He's a cardiologist," she protested.

"So?"

"I'm not looking for deep feelings. It's just sex with no strings attached. If Spencer is as shallow as you say, he's perfect. Walking away won't be a problem. And don't be using the double standard on me. Guys do it all the time."

Nick turned his back on the nursery window. If she were a guy, he wouldn't be tied in knots right now. Thoughts of her—specifically, thoughts of her naked—had kept him awake last night. Maintaining their friendship after the divorce had been an extraordinarily pleasant surprise. He liked talking to her, keeping in touch without having to see her and not be able to touch. It was comfortable and he didn't want to lose that. So he'd forced himself to think about her platonically.

Then she had to go and ask him to be the father of her baby and he couldn't stop thinking about every last inch of her body, from the sexy column of her neck to the rogue freckle on the back of her knee. Did he want to sleep with her? Hell, yes. But a baby?

He'd screwed up their marriage, and the best thing he'd been able to say was that no kids were involved. It was his fault they hadn't worked. From the outside he looked like a workaholic, but the truth was he had never been "all in" with his feelings. The way his father had fallen apart after his mother walked out was like watching the Rock of Gibraltar crumble into dust. Nick would never let himself lose control like that.

But that line in the sand meant he couldn't meet Ryleigh's needs and their marriage had been a casualty. As he recognized the longing in her eyes while looking at the babies, the guilt and responsibility of marrying when he knew he'd never be able to give her enough, weighed heavily on him. He'd really hurt her.

"I don't expect you to understand, Nick." Her voice

wobbled. "I may never have a baby, but I have to stop the hurt inside whenever I see one. The only way to do that is to try. I don't want to make the same mistake I did with our marriage."

"You didn't do anything," he said.

"You're wrong. I didn't try as hard as I could have." She looked up at him, tears swimming in her eyes. "Don't be alarmed, but I think I'm going to cry. So I'll just be going now."

Something cracked and crumbled inside him as he reluctantly reached out and pulled her into his arms. No matter how hard he tried, he hadn't been able to dismiss what she'd said about a man's need for sex rivaling a woman's yearning for a baby. It convinced him as nothing else could have that she was determined to move this plan forward, with or without him.

He hadn't been able to give her what she needed when they were married. But now he could give her what she wanted and maybe cancel out at least one of the black marks on his soul.

"So you're sure about this baby thing," he said.

"Absolutely." Conviction rang in her voice in spite of the tears.

Good for her. Nick was only sure about one thing. He couldn't stand by and watch. He had no idea what form hell would take, but for sure he was going there because he couldn't stand the thought of Ryleigh with another man. The very idea made him angrier than it should have and more pissed off than he'd ever been in his life.

"Okay," he said. "Count me in."

Chapter Two

Ryleigh walked through the parking lot of Peretti's Italian Restaurant with Nick's hand at the small of her back. It wasn't the touch alone that had memories crashing in on her, although the way his fingers had her nerves tingling was annoying. But the déjà vu-ish feeling was more about this being their favorite restaurant. Their *place*. In another life.

He'd brought her here on their first date and swore she'd love it as much as he did. She'd barely eaten anything. Too nervous. Too love struck. Too anxious to sleep with him, be with him, which had happened maybe thirty minutes after they'd left that night. They couldn't keep their hands off each other or be in each other's arms fast enough.

A few months later Nick had asked her to marry him in the corner booth at the back of this restaurant.

"Dr. Nick. Mrs. Nick." Vito Peretti's slightly accented voice just kept the nostalgia hits coming. A handsome

Italian man in his fifties, he smiled as they stepped inside the door.

"Hi, Vito."

He'd taken a shine to a young couple in love. "It has been a long time since I see you together. Dr. Nick alone is wrong. I am so happy that two of my favorite people are back together."

"No. We're not together. I mean, we're together right now. This moment." Ryleigh slid her hands into the pockets of her black slacks. "We just came in to eat. Things to discuss."

"Excellent. First you talk." Vito nodded at Nick. "Clear the air. Fix the problem."

"Just dinner," Nick answered.

"Whatever you say." The restaurant owner winked. "Food first. Then romance."

Not this time, Ryleigh thought. She was over Nick Damian. That's what made her plan workable.

Through the dimly lighted restaurant they were led to the back and she knew what was coming.

"Your table," Vito said.

Every memory cell inside her vibrated in protest, but protesting for real would just raise more questions. When Vito pulled the white-cloth-covered table out for them to slide into the rounded booth, she did so without uttering a word. And, equally silent, Nick sat next to her. But the muscle in his jaw moved.

"I will bring your favorite wine," he said.

Cabernet, she remembered. Some French name that never stuck in her head. Before she could tell him not to bother because she needed her wits intact, the man disappeared.

Nick rubbed a hand across the back of his neck. His eyes seemed to turn down at the corners more than usual, a clear indication that he was tired. He'd changed out of the scrubs she'd seen him wearing earlier that day outside the newborn nursery, when he agreed to her plan.

Now he had on worn jeans, a long-sleeved white cotton shirt and battered brown leather jacket. It was October and the brutal summer heat was gone, making the days pleasant but the nights chilly. One of the things she'd missed most was his warmth in bed. Then again, half the time he hadn't been there. Why had it been so damn hard to get over what she hardly ever had?

"Sorry about Vito," he said.

"No. I'm sorry. If my place wasn't such a disaster from moving across the country, I'd have invited you over."

"Still, I didn't think it through. I guess it was a muscle-memory thing. With you in the car, it sort of just steered its way over here."

Part of her hoped that meant he hadn't brought another woman here. The other part recognized that feeling was stupid and foolish.

"No big deal. I'm just so grateful you agreed to help me out. We have things to discuss and the least I can do is buy you dinner."

"I'll arm wrestle you when the check comes." One dark eyebrow lifted. "Although you might want to rethink that offer. A budget is your friend when having a baby."

"You are having a baby?" Vito stopped at their table and heard the last couple words. "There is no fooling me. I can spot lovers, no?" Then he frowned. "But a pregnant lady should not consume alcohol. Perhaps instead of a bottle just a glass for Dr. Nick. And sparkling cider for Mrs. Nick?"

She wasn't Mrs. Nick anymore. And after all this, Ryleigh was prepared to tackle Vito if he tried to leave without pouring her at least one glass out of that bottle of cabernet.

"I'm not pregnant," she said.

"No worry." Vito shrugged. "So you are here to set a mood as you try."

She started to say no and realized that was only half true. They weren't here to get their mood on as much as talk about getting pregnant. But she had a feeling if she talked about talking, Vito would remind her that verbal communication was not the way to get the job done.

"We'd appreciate it if you'd open the bottle," Nick said.

"With pleasure. And your Caesar salad will be served shortly."

"But—"

The man held up his hand, then poured a glass of wine for each of them. "I remember your favorites. A salad to share. Bread sticks with marinara and alfredo sauces for dipping. Then Vito's world famous lasagna, also to share. And tiramisu for dessert." He winked. "You share everything."

More memories crashed over her. He was right about all of it.

"You have to give him credit. Nothing wrong with his powers of recall." Nick grinned and held up his wine. "To Vito."

She clinked her glass to his. "Gotta love him."

"So, you're not settled yet?" He rested his forearm on the table.

"I'm renting a two-bedroom hospital-subsidized apartment until I can find something more permanent. I have a lot of stuff in storage."

"Anything I can do to help?"

Only with the baby. She hoped he hadn't changed his

mind about that. But there was something else she remembered about Nick. Once he'd given his word, he wouldn't go back on it. "That's why we're here."

"The baby."

"Yeah," she agreed. "Or, more specifically, the rules of engagement."

"Okay. Go."

She thought for a moment. "First of all, I need to say that I don't want to lose your friendship. So, if that's going to be a problem, speak now—"

"Agreed." But his blue eyes turned a little dark and broody.

"We need to keep it simple and uncomplicated. Although Vito will be disappointed about no romance. But that's the best way to mess up a wonderful friendship."

"That works for me."

"No matter what," she added emphatically.

"Do you want me to pinkie swear?" he asked, holding up his little finger.

"If that's a guarantee—yes," she said, crooking hers and curving it around his outstretched finger.

"Okay. What else?"

She dropped her hand into her lap as she thought. "That's the only rule that comes to mind."

He smiled. "Did that feel too easy to you?"

"Give me a minute. I'll think of something to make problems. Oh, right, about why we're here." Between the wine and his teasing, she began to relax. "I need to do some research on the internet about how to conceive a baby."

Nick's eyes sparkled with amusement over the top of the glass as he sipped his wine. "Unless anatomy or the mechanics of procreation have changed since I went to med school, conception is probably achieved in the usual way."

"Funny guy."

Not.

Their shoulders brushed and tingles of awareness danced through her. Her skin was hot, sensitive and she was pretty sure that was about anticipation. Getting naked with Nick was never far from her mind since she'd decided he should father her baby. And it was worse after walking into Peretti's. Like he'd said, muscle memory.

"You used to appreciate my sense of humor," he reminded her.

"I still do." It was one of her favorite things about him. "Let me be more specific. I want to find out the optimum time of the month. To conceive. And anything else that might increase the odds of achieving the desired objective."

"If you'd like, I can talk to Rebecca Hamilton."

Aside from the fact that their agreement wasn't for public consumption, she didn't really want him talking to another woman about her and the baby. "Is that your girlfriend?"

"She's a girl. And she's a friend who's married. Also a doctor. Ob-gyn. Any information you need, I'm sure she'll have."

"Oh." Ryleigh refused to believe the ugly feeling churning through her had anything to do with jealousy. "Maybe. But are you prepared to answer her questions about why you're asking?"

"Not really."

Was his voice just a tiny bit hoarse? His eyes narrowed and more intense than moments ago? The expression reminded her of how he looked when he wanted her. A woman who'd craved even the barest amount of attention from the man she was completely in love with wasn't likely to forget the look on his face when he wanted her.

Ryleigh cleared her throat. "Okay, so how about this. I'll do my research and we'll regroup."

"Just let me know when and where," he said.

"Give me a couple days. My place next time. It's near the hospital so that will be convenient for us both."

"I'll be there."

There might have been eagerness in his tone or it could just be wishful thinking on her part. It had happened before. Once upon a time she'd mistaken his wanting her as a sign that he reciprocated her feelings because she'd so desperately hoped he would. Now she knew better, but knowing better didn't stop the hitch in her breathing, the pumped-up pulse. If just thinking about sex made her feel like this, what would actual sex do?

Make a baby, she hoped.

And that would be the end of it. No strings attached. Love had made everything difficult, but she'd learned her lesson and wasn't going there again. That ship had sailed. But attraction was a different story. She was still attracted to Nick and that was a good thing.

It would help when the time came to get her pregnant.

Several days later, at the appointed time, Nick knocked on Ryleigh's door. Her place was on the second floor located in an apartment complex behind Mercy Medical Center. He'd just finished up evening rounds and his two patients were doing well. Barring complications, he expected to discharge them the next morning.

The anticipation of seeing his ex-wife tonight had hummed through him all day. He hadn't missed her these last two years, not exactly. Every time the idea of it crept in, he shut the feeling down. But now that she was back, well it was safe to say he was in a pretty good mood. More than one person had commented on that today and it was probably not a coincidence that all of them were women.

The door opened, and there was the one woman who'd occupied more of his thoughts than he was comfortable with. "Ryleigh."

"Hi, Nick. Come in." She stepped back and opened the door wider. After he walked in, she shut it behind him. "This place is still a mess. Sorry."

"Don't be. Not on my account."

There were moving boxes stacked around the perimeter of the room and several on the dinette just off the kitchen. He stood in the living room with its charmless beige couch and matching chair. There was a faux-wood coffee table and matching end tables with ugly orange ceramic lamp, times two. "Don't tell me. The place came furnished."

"Pretty hideous, huh?"

"I didn't say that."

"Not in so many words."

But looking at Ryleigh cancelled out the unattractive stuff. In worn jeans that hugged her curves and a pale yellow sweater she was like a slice of sunshine. Her shiny hair was pulled back in a ponytail and gold hoops dangled from her ears. As good as his mood had been, it got better still, just staring at her.

She sighed. "I had delusions of actually cooking, but work and research got in the way. How do you feel about Chinese takeout?"

"I'm easy."

"Good. The food cartons, plates and eating utensils are in the kitchen. Help yourself. I'll get drinks. We'll eat in here."

He walked in the kitchen and saw all his favorite Chinese food on display. Spring rolls. Sweet and sour chicken. Chow mein. A fork and one set of chopsticks. He'd tried to teach her how to use them and smiled at the memory of flying food and her swearing. But that was then and this was now. Ryleigh and Nick, Part Two. Simple, uncomplicated sex. Guys would kill to be in his shoes.

He set his plate down on one of the paper towels on the coffee table. Place mats. How very Ryleigh of her. She brought him a club soda with lime.

"I figured you were on call."

"Yeah." He always was and it left no time for them when they were married.

"I'm not."

She set a glass of white wine beside his drink and settled next to him on the couch. They ate in silence and it wasn't awkward. It was nice. Felt like old times.

"How was your day?" she asked.

"Good. You?"

"I'm settling in. Lots of meetings. Strategizing about new and creative ways to raise money for Children's Medical Charities. It's a challenge in this economy."

"If anyone can talk the people into parting with their money, it's you." Nick should know. She'd somehow convinced him to go along with this baby thing.

When they finished eating she cleared the plates, refilled their drinks, then went down the hall and brought back a bunch of file folders from the second bedroom she used as a home office.

She put the tall stack of paperwork on the coffee table then sat beside him again. "My research."

"No wonder you fed me first. To keep up my strength."

"Having a baby isn't as easy as you might think." Her cocoa-colored eyes danced with laughter.

"And here I thought it was all about biology."

"That. And timing. It's critical." She opened a file. "But there are things that can boost the odds of conceiving."

"Such as?"

"The goal is to fertilize the egg."

"Yeah. I think that was covered in Birds and Bees 101." He moved closer, glancing at her computer printout, but mostly to feel the warmth of her. Draw in the sweet floral fragrance of her skin. That was something he'd missed and it hadn't responded to the shut-down-feelings therapy.

"Everyone can use a refresher course. Even you, Doctor." She looked at her notes. "Ovulation is the key. Besides guessing about when it occurs, there are ovulation predictor kits available at the pharmacy and basal-body-temperature-charts to know when it's happening."

"Really?"

All this fell into her territory and he didn't need to know. But he liked watching her when she talked, the intensity and enthusiasm. The combination made her so damn beautiful he could hardly breathe. Still, this wasn't about him. The amount of time and effort she'd put into this was a clear indication of how deep her desire to have a baby.

"When you pee on the stick from a kit, it will turn purple the day before ovulation, indicating a surge in…" She stopped and read from the paper. "Luteinizing hormone, which is what causes the ovary to release an egg. The key is to time sex within a day of the LH surge."

Nick was focused on her mouth and pretty much didn't hear much of anything until she said "sex." He didn't need a predictor kit or a thermometer to know he had a surge of his own *and* a spike in body temp.

He said the only thing he could think of, what with

the blood flowing south of his belt. "Science is pretty amazing."

"And fascinating."

"Anything else I need to know?" Like when and where. Now was okay with him. He took a sip of water and not because he was thirsty.

"There was some information about positions during sex."

He nearly choked. "Oh?"

"Yeah. Missionary might be more promising, but there aren't any studies to back it up."

If Ryleigh was involved, he'd be willing to volunteer for research on the subject. "Okay. I can see where that would be practical."

"Then I saw something about lying still afterward. Remaining horizontal for fifteen minutes." She shuffled through the papers, looking embarrassed and pretty damn cute. "Again, there's no evidence to support the theory that it makes a difference, but it can't hurt, either."

So, a woman's inclination to cuddle afterward might be based in biology and science, not emotion, he thought. "Got it."

"I found a website with frequently asked questions."

"Okay, now I'm starting to get performance anxiety."

She slid to her corner of the couch and tucked her legs up beside her. A flush crept into her cheeks, and she didn't quite meet his eyes.

She crossed her arms at her waist. "There was some discussion about a woman achieving climax—to increase the chances of conceiving."

No pressure.

"And?" When she hesitated, he said, "Don't tell me. There are no studies."

She laughed. "No. But there's a belief that the contractions move the guys along toward the target."

"It makes sense."

But he could truthfully say that not once when he'd made love to her had his goal been to move the guys. He'd only ever wanted to hold her in his arms, make her happy. And he was pretty sure he'd succeeded in bed. In every other way, he'd failed her, which was why making things up to her now was so important.

She lifted her gaze for a moment. "And last but not least there's the debate about a.m. or p.m."

"Morning or night—what?"

"Sex." She sat cross-legged and leaned forward. "Studies have been done on this one and some indicate that there are more swimmers in the morning. But only a million, give or take. Fairly insignificant."

"Hey, that's my guys you're talking about."

"I didn't mean to insinuate." She smiled, and the way her eyes lit up tied him in knots. "The thing is that when you're talking eighty-eight million as opposed to eighty-seven million, it sounds like a lot but really isn't."

"I actually knew that only one is required." Was it just him, or was it hot in here?

"Right."

His gaze slid past hers to the bare walls, stack of boxes and unattractive, serviceable furniture. She was a nester and looked out of place in this cracker box with ugly furniture. It was just wrong. Fixing people was what he did, and the words popped out of his mouth before he'd thought them through.

"Move in with me."

She blinked and sat up straighter. "What?"

"To achieve your objective, timing is everything. If that predictor stick turns purple, your body temp goes up and nature is good to go, what happens if you're here and I'm there?" He shrugged. "It's the classic setup for missed opportunities."

"There's some logic to that, but I don't know, Nick." She caught her lip between her teeth, the very first time she'd looked indecisive. "Invading your space?"

Her lack of enthusiasm made him want to convince her even more. "It was your space, too." He'd gotten the house in the divorce. "There's plenty of room, as you know. And we don't want to drag out the process, right?"

"Yes, but—"

"Like science, nature and biology it's practical."

He phrased it the same way she had. Distantly. As if they were talking about another couple being intimate.

Nick remembered all the messy emotions that had nearly brought him down right after she'd left. A guy puts up armor and when a girl gets through it leaves a mark. But this was different. The rules had been discussed and all parties involved agreed. Distanced. Simple. Goal-oriented. She'd get what she wanted. His guilt would be erased. Win/win. Both of them could move on. No feelings, no mess.

"Don't you want to maximize the chances of conception?" he asked.

"Yes." She met his gaze and her own was dark with determination. "More than anything in the world I want to have a baby."

"Well, then?"

"I've done the menstrual math. The old-fashioned way," she added. "By my calculations ovulation is about a week away. Next Monday."

"So I'll help you move in Saturday. You don't want heavy lifting to shock your eggs or anything. Relax the rest of the weekend."

"You're sure about this?" she asked skeptically.

"Yeah." The gate on his feelings opened for a split second and excitement leaked out.

"Okay, then. I'll move in."

Nick nodded and again his gaze was drawn to the boxes around the room. She'd said it was a mess and only now did he realize that was a metaphor for his life. He hadn't really expected her to take him up on his offer to move in, but there was no denying he was far too pleased that she had.

In about a week they were going to do what a man and woman did to make a baby. He was pretty pleased about that, too.

Chapter Three

Ryleigh stopped her compact car behind Nick's silver SUV at the gated entrance to the neighborhood. She watched him lean out the driver's window and speak to the guard, then cock his thumb toward her, obviously explaining that she would be living with him. That there was no need to call out the SWAT team on her account.

When the SUV pulled forward, she followed, then stopped when the guard held up his hand.

She lowered her window. "Hi."

"Miss Evans." This man was different from the one who'd worked the gate when she lived here. He was young, twenty something and wearing a light blue uniform shirt with navy-colored, official-looking emblems. "Doctor Damian explained that you'll be staying with him."

"That's right." But only for well-timed sex.

He handed her a visitor's pass. "Just put this on your dashboard and you're good to go—or stay."

"Thanks."

"Have a nice evening."

"You, too," she said, displaying the cardboard square where he'd directed.

This was the first time she'd been back since they'd broken up, and driving through the community was surreal. Nothing had changed, but everything felt different. The houses were all large, expensive and well-maintained. But it wasn't familiar. She felt distant. And sad. She'd really loved the house and this area.

She pulled into the circular drive, parking behind Nick's car. He was standing beside it. Glancing at the stately, two-story house brought on that surreal feeling again, but really she'd been wearing that hat ever since she'd presented her how-to-conceive-in-a-nanosecond research.

As far as bizarre moments went, that topped the list. But she'd felt it important to mention everything that could possibly expedite the process. She wanted to get pregnant right away for lots of reasons, not the least of which was not to see Nick after mission accomplished. It didn't seem prudent to tempt fate too far what with her attraction to him still going on. The only way she'd managed to get through her sex notes was by keeping the conversation clinical and detached, as if she were talking about someone else.

But it wasn't someone else temporarily moving into Nick's house. It was her, the same woman who'd moved into this place seeing everything by the light of the stars in her eyes and the delusion that they were going to be blissfully happy there for the rest of their lives. She wasn't sure which philosopher said the only thing we could count on was change, but the time came when she'd wanted to choke him. She hated change. It was almost always bad.

Bliss and happiness were elusive and highly overrated.

Living in the real world wasn't as much fun, but the highs and lows were smoothed out into straight and steady. She could live with straight and steady.

Blowing out a cleansing breath, she opened her car door and stepped onto the concrete drive separating the house from the landscaping. The dry riverbed running through the length of the yard was still dry and lined with smooth rocks. It was bordered by gold and purple flowering lantana bushes. Everything looked just as it had when she'd left. Nothing had changed but her.

"Why don't I take your things inside?" Nick said.

His deep voice from behind startled her out of the bittersweet reverie. She turned and forced a big smile. "Sounds like a plan."

After she unlocked her trunk and started to pull out her suitcase, he put a hand on hers.

"I'll get it. I'm pretty sure it hasn't gotten any lighter since I put it in there."

"Thanks."

His palm was big and strong, his fingers warm. The touch had heat pooling in her belly and flushing her cheeks. Twilight had dropped shadows over the craggy mountains not so far away, and she was pretty sure Nick couldn't see how the brush of his hand affected her.

That was something else that hadn't changed. But attraction without emotion was like a bow without an arrow—no power to wound.

It took several trips to carry suitcases, garment bags and toiletries into the house. He'd suggested she stay here while looking for a permanent place of her own and she'd brought a lot of clothes with her. The apartment was utilitarian and good for storage, but she'd be more comfortable in a house.

Looking around the two-story entry, she wasn't so sure.

Memories attacked from every direction. Nick carrying her over the threshold when they bought the place. The huge kitchen with granite countertops was especially bittersweet. He'd made love to her beside the stainless-steel refrigerator because his eyes went smoky, her insides turned liquid and they simply couldn't hold back. In fact, the day they moved in he'd declared his intention to make love to her in every room of the house. They'd nearly met that challenge.

She scanned the family room with its big flat-screen TV and the dark green corner group in front of it. In spite of all her efforts to stop it, a big sigh leaked out.

Nick stopped beside her. "Are you okay?"

"Fine." Afraid he would see the lie, she didn't look at him. "Why?"

"You're awfully quiet."

"Just checking out the old stomping grounds."

He rested his hands on lean hips. His jeans were worn nearly white in the most interesting places. The long sleeves of his navy-blue shirt were rolled up, revealing wide wrists and a dusting of dark hair on his forearms. He always dressed casually, and right now was no exception. It also wasn't an indication of whether or not he was working. He'd told her Carlton Gallagher was on call today, and she wondered if she should feel honored. Maybe tomorrow.

"And?"

"What?" She was a little disturbed by how easily one look at him could annihilate her concentration.

"How does it look? Your old stomping grounds."

"The same," she answered truthfully. "I was just remembering how festive everything was at Christmas."

The corners of his mouth turned up. "You mean with the tree in here instead of the living room?"

"Yeah."

"I stand by what I said then."

"As do I." She could feel the warmth from his body and smell the slightly spicy scent of his skin. Quivers started inside her and rippled everywhere. Bumping up against the bittersweet recollections. "The decorated tree would have been fabulous in the front window as people drove by and looked at the outside decorations."

"But we wouldn't have enjoyed it." He held out his hand and indicated the large room. "Here, we could see it along with a fire in the fireplace, watching TV, or eating dinner."

His insistence was ironic since he'd hardly ever been there for dinner, nights in front of the fire, or watching TV together. But that was water under the bridge.

"You won. We did it your way." She'd given in because making him happy was her goal. Now it was her turn to get what she wanted.

"Other than that, how does it look?" he asked.

"The same. And I'm a little surprised."

"Redecorating isn't my thing." The teasing tone was missing from his voice.

Was he feeling nostalgic, too? Not the Nick she remembered.

"That's not what I meant." She looked up at him. "I'm surprised you didn't sell the house after the divorce."

"I had my reasons."

The dark look in his eyes made her wonder. "Such as?"

"I didn't get around to it, then the housing market tanked. Moving is time-consuming and it really doesn't much matter where I get my mail."

All practical reasons, she thought. If the situation had been reversed, she'd have sold it at a loss simply because it was too painful to share the space with the ghosts of what would never be.

"And I'm hardly ever here," he added.

That wasn't new information. It was time to move forward. Literally.

"So," she said brightly. "Where do you want me?"

A sexy smile turned up the corners of his mouth. "Do I get a vote?"

She didn't have to ask where his thoughts had gone. That made two of them, but she wasn't here for *that* sex. This wasn't personal.

"I meant which bedroom."

"Take your pick," he said. "Although there's not really much of a choice."

She walked upstairs to check it out for herself. The master bedroom was off the landing at the top. She peeked inside at the four-poster bed, matching oak dresser and armoire. A pair of running shoes beside the walk-in closet and a towel carelessly tossed on a corner chair indicated he still slept in here.

Ryleigh moved past the doorway and peeked into the room beside it. "This would make a great nursery."

"That's what you said the first time you saw the house." His voice was husky.

That wasn't something she would have expected him to remember, and the sweetness of it made her chest tight. "It's a good-size room, close to the master. If the baby cried, one of us would have heard."

"So you said."

But it was still empty, a reflection of what her marriage had become. Not at all like her romanticized vision before she'd realized that being in love by herself wasn't working for her.

She quickly checked out the other three bedrooms and

realized he was right about not having choices. The room farthest away from Nick's was the only one furnished. She'd wanted a comfortable guest room, just in case they needed it and had started decorating there. In her plan, the others could wait for the babies they were going to have. But plans changed and the family never happened.

"I'll take this one," she finally said.

"I figured."

He went back downstairs for her things and she was glad to be alone. How ironic was that? She'd never felt like that when this was her home. So now she was over the first hurdle, the one she'd dreaded most. Facing down the past. Part of her had wanted to turn down Nick's offer to stay here, but that would have given it importance, adding complication and breaking their cardinal rule.

Now she'd walked down memory lane and somehow felt more whole. Stronger. Unlike the immature girl who'd lived here before, she was a woman going after what she wanted. Until zero hour, she'd be sleeping as far from Nick as she could get. With luck it was far enough to keep any more memories from following.

On the up side—she and Nick never had sex in the guest room.

The night after moving into Nick's place, Ryleigh juggled a pizza box in her hands, then rang the doorbell of her friend's condo. Almost immediately it was opened and Avery O'Neill stood there in jeans and a royal-blue sweater. She had blue eyes, a blond pixie haircut that was incredibly flattering and she barely weighed a hundred pounds soaking wet. At just over five feet, she was shorter than Ryleigh. Almost no one was shorter than her. This woman was too cute for words, but Ryleigh didn't hold that against her. They were best friends.

"Hey, you."

"Hey you back."

"Get in here." Avery pulled the door open wider and took the pizza. She walked the length of the extensive tiled entryway and into the kitchen. The white cupboards topped with black granite were a big, bold look for her pretty petite friend. After setting down the box, she opened her arms. "Now for a proper welcome-home hug."

Ryleigh squeezed her hard, then held her at arm's length and studied the new look. "Love the hair."

"Thanks."

"It makes you look like a fairy, like you belong in a Harry Potter or Lord of the Rings book."

"Spencer Stone calls me Tinker Bell."

The doctor was the finest cardiologist at Mercy Medical Center and Nick's best friend. Ryleigh still remembered the look on his face when he thought she planned to approach the guy to father her baby. It could have been jealousy. A girl could hope anyway. But probably it was just shock.

Her friend was the hospital controller and handled the day-to-day hospital money issues. They'd met when Ryleigh was executive assistant to the administrator. "Is Doctor Drop-Dead-Gorgeous still giving you a hard time about all the cardio equipment he wants to buy for Mercy Medical Center?"

"Always," her friend said.

"If he was a pediatric cardiologist I might be able to help you out. But he's a big-people doctor."

"Yes, he is. And likes to brag that he fixes broken hearts."

"He does."

"And he's good at it," Avery admitted grudgingly. "If he weren't it would be a lot easier to dislike him."

"But you manage?"

Her friend shrugged. "He hits on women like crash dummies hit windshields."

"And that's a problem?"

"Not for me. I can handle him."

Ryleigh didn't doubt that. She might look small, blonde, fragile and defenseless, but Avery was not an airhead, didn't take any crap and could handle pretty much anything.

She pulled two paper plates out of the pantry and scooped a piece of pepperoni pizza onto each one. Then she carried the food into the adjacent family room and set it on the glass-topped table sitting between the green and coral floral sofa and the fireplace with wall-mounted flat-screen TV above.

"Well, I like your new look. It's adorable and becoming. Fresh and new since I last saw you."

"Barely four months ago when I visited you in Baltimore."

"I know that tone." Ryleigh followed her and sat on the couch. "You're annoyed."

"Yes, I am." After filling two glasses with red wine, Avery sat beside her.

"Why?"

"Let me count the ways." Avery held up her index finger. "First, you moved away."

Ryleigh finished chewing a bite of pizza, but it tasted like cardboard. She knew where this conversation was headed. "You know why I had to leave."

"I know you believed it would save your marriage, but I think we can all see how well that turned out."

"Sounds stupid when you say it like that, but distance seemed like a good idea at the time." She sipped her wine, but it didn't dull the memory of how much it had hurt to leave Nick. "I know now that I was hoping he would beg me not to go. Even after I'd started the job, I had a fantasy that he'd come after me, bring me back. It was immature and naive."

"Nope. I completely get it." There was sympathy in her friend's blue eyes. "I just didn't like it."

"That's why I love you."

"Really?" The annoyed tone was back. "If that were true, you'd have said something about moving back to Las Vegas. No?"

"No. When you visited, I'd just applied for the job and you know how that goes. Contact followed by weeks of waiting. An interview and more waiting. Another interview, then the field is narrowed to two and you're on pins and needles while they try to decide, even though we all know they're probably going to flip a coin. Heads it's John Doe, tails it's Ryleigh Evans."

"I know how it works, but best friends tell each other everything."

Ryleigh wanted to remind her that there was a big chunk of her life that Avery wouldn't talk about, but decided not to go there. There must be a damn good reason why she didn't talk about it, and the best friend bond respected that.

"And sometimes," Ryleigh said, "a friend tries to spare her best friend pain. I didn't want to get your hopes up and then have it all fall apart."

"Okay. Totally understandable. Because my hopes would have gone stratosphere high. And I remember how hard it was to let you go. I still haven't forgiven you for leaving."

"You just said you understood."

"I did and I do. But that's different from letting you off the hook for abandoning me."

"Well, I'm back now."

"Yes, you are and about darn time. But why is that?" Annoyance was gone, replaced by curiosity.

"Because I'm the regional coordinator for Children's Medical Charities."

"Uh-huh."

"It's a really good job."

"Totally," Avery agreed.

"And very important."

"You'll get no argument from me."

"Doesn't feel that way," Ryleigh pointed out. "I'm raising money for programs and equipment to help kids."

"I know what the charity does. You'll do a fantastic job because you're motivated. No one loves kids more than you." Avery finished her pizza, then tapped her lip thoughtfully. "As I recall, you were determined to have a baby before the big 3-0. How's that going?"

This is where the best-friend bond got awkward. Confessing everything would result in Avery's honest opinion. And most of the time Ryleigh valued that. Now? Well, no one wanted to be told they were an idiot. Or worse, crazy.

Ryleigh rolled up her empty paper plate. "Oh, you know."

"If I knew, I wouldn't have asked. What's going on? And don't tell me nothing. This is me and I know better."

"Power down, O'Neill. You're right." She sighed. "I actively looked for a job in Las Vegas after coming to the realization that Nick is the best man I know and I want him to father my baby."

Avery blinked and stared, speechless for several moments. "The desert heat has cooked your brain cells."

"It's October and not hot. I think you just called me crazy."

"No. I'd never say that. But, Ryleigh—" She shook her head. "What are you thinking?"

"That my biological clock is ticking. I don't want to take my chances at a sperm bank, and men who are good father material don't grow on trees. The ones I was meeting just didn't measure up and I'm not getting any younger."

"But Nick is your ex."

"So? That doesn't mean he isn't good looking. Or smart. He's a doctor and treats kids with breathing problems. Doesn't get any better than that."

"He *is* a tough act to follow, I'll grant you that. But your ex?" Avery said again.

"Not being able to love me isn't a deal-breaking biological flaw."

Avery put her empty paper plate on the coffee table and grabbed her wineglass. "Does Nick know any of this?"

"All of it."

"And after he requested a psych evaluation?"

"Stop calling me crazy." But Ryleigh understood this was coming from a place of sincerity and caring.

"Did I say the 'c' word? It did not come out of my mouth. And don't keep me in suspense. What was his reaction?"

In for a penny, in for a pound. "He asked me to move in with him. To make the logistics more—logistical. During my fertile time." When her friend was quiet, she begged, "Say something, Avery."

"How did you talk him into it? Not the moving-in thing, the fathering thing."

"I think he feels guilty. For his part of what went wrong in our marriage. But there were also tears involved. I just couldn't help it when I saw the babies in the nursery. And he happened to be there."

Ryleigh hadn't faked the emotion and couldn't be sorry

it helped convince him. But she'd never forget how good his arms had felt around her. The comfort he'd offered without hesitation. She had no illusion that it came from anywhere besides friendship, but that didn't diminish her appreciation.

Avery nodded thoughtfully, processing everything. There was a gleam in her blue eyes when she asked, "You know that having a baby with Nick will require you to have sex with him?"

"Yes. That's part of the logistics. So when I'm—you know—he'll be…you know."

"Handy?"

"Yeah."

The expression in her friend's eyes turned the tiniest bit wicked. "So you haven't done it yet?"

"No. Not quite the right time in my cycle."

"And I'm going to be Auntie Avery?"

"With a little luck."

"And sex." Her expression turned serious. "This is me and I'm there for you. Whatever you need. Count on it."

"I have no doubt about that." Ryleigh knew there was more. "But?"

"I saw what you went through when you and Nick fell apart. I held you when you cried. What kind of friend would I be if I didn't help you look at this whole thing from every angle?"

"Just spit it out," Ryleigh said.

"Okay. I have to ask. Do you really think you can go through with this and come out unscathed?"

"By 'this,' I'm assuming you mean sex without complications." When her friend nodded she said, "Men do it all the time."

"If God wanted women to be like men, He'd have given us the same equipment. If you have sex with Nick, I'm pretty sure there will be feelings involved. On your part, anyway. I just don't want you to get hurt again."

"I won't."

"Famous last words."

"Don't you see, Avery? From the time I was a little girl, I've wanted to be a mother. I want it more than I can put into words and it's this close." She held up her thumb and index fingers, a fraction of an inch apart. "Please don't rain on my parade."

"That's the last thing I'd do." Avery finished the wine in her glass and set it on the table. She slid closer and leaned in for a hug before saying, "I love the idea of you having a baby, getting what you want. And I'm serious about having aunt status. I just want to make sure you know what you're doing with Nick."

"I appreciate that and if it were you, I'd feel the same way." Her friend's eyes darkened for a moment, and she quickly added, "Don't worry. I've thought this through." Ryleigh met the other woman's gaze. "I've been there, done that. Now I'm over him. Nick can't hurt me, which makes him the perfect guy."

And by her calculations, the perfect time in her cycle was tomorrow.

Chapter Four

Today was Monday.

Nick got out of the shower and dried himself off, then tied the towel around his waist while he shaved—a habit left over from when he was married.

Normally Monday was his least favorite day, as it was for most people. But his schedule wasn't like most people's and he often saw patients seven days a week, blurring them all together.

Except Monday.

That's when the paperwork, billing and loose ends from a busy weekend had to be managed and cleaned up. Between seeing sick kids in his office and the ones admitted to the hospital, the hours from nine to five were all spoken for. That left the evening to sort out everything else.

At least this Monday would start out better than most. If the smell of coffee drifting to him was anything to go by, Ryleigh was in the kitchen. He'd missed her last night when she'd gone to see Avery. Stupid to miss her. He'd pushed the feeling away after she moved to the East Coast. Why would it get through now when she was back? But questioning the why of it didn't make the reality any less true.

She'd been living with him—correction: she'd been living under his roof—for two days, and one evening without her had felt lonelier than any he could remember since the divorce. In hindsight, asking her to move in was probably a bonehead move, but there was no way to undo it without looking like a complete ass. He wasn't willing to go there.

He combed his hair, spritzed cologne on his bare chest, then dressed in jeans and a cotton shirt. It was his belief that a suit and tie intimidated little kids, or maybe that was just rationalization. Either way he was comfortable.

At least he was until walking into the kitchen. His body went hot and hard at the sight of Ryleigh. Her back was to him, but she had a pretty spectacular rear view. She was wearing a red suit and four-inch come-and-get-me heels. The skirt probably hit her just above the knee and left what seemed like a mile of leg showing. Her shiny brown hair teased the jacket collar and he ached to nudge the silky strands aside and kiss her neck.

She used to moan and quiver, then rotate into his arms when he did that. This was one of those times that hindsight was twenty/twenty. He hadn't kissed her neck often enough when he'd had the chance and the right.

Moving farther into the room, he cleared his throat. "Hey."

"Good morning." She glanced over her shoulder. "Want coffee?"

"Yeah. Thanks."

She poured some into two mugs, then brought one to

him where he stood by the granite-topped center island. Her black leather Coach purse was there with her red cell phone beside it.

"Here you go."

He took the cup and blew on the steaming liquid before taking a sip. "Good. Better than mine."

"That coffee maker hardly looks used. Do you even make any for yourself?"

"Not much," he admitted. "I usually have it at the office or the hospital."

But having it with her was so much better. Maybe the taste wasn't so excellent as much as just looking at her sweet, fresh, beautiful face made it seem that way.

"I picked up a few healthy food items from the grocery store." Ryleigh set her mug beside her cell phone. "And I'm making oatmeal. Want some?"

"Is that a trick question?"

"No trick." A laugh bubbled out as she pulled a pot from under the cupboard beneath the cooktop. "I'm fixing it anyway. I'll double the amount if you're interested."

He was interested all right, but not in dry oats hydrated with water. "I'd rather poke myself in the eye with a sharp stick."

"I bet if there was bacon, sausage, ham or steak involved your attitude would be different."

"You'd win that bet because none of the above have the taste and characteristics of wallpaper paste."

In a warning gesture, she shook a wooden spoon at him. "One of these days, Doctor, your cholesterol and triglycerides will go through the roof and you'll be singing a different tune."

"I'm willing to risk it."

She shrugged. "Your body."

True enough, and it was much more interested in hers.

The fitted jacket hugged her waist and hips like a lover's hands. He'd seen her naked and some things you couldn't un-see just because the marriage was over. Too many times to count, a vision of her in his bed wearing nothing but a sexy smile had haunted his thoughts, filled his dreams.

But not once in the visions had she been standing in front of a stove stirring mush. Although he liked having her there, it would have been nicer if she'd been doing it minus the red suit and anything she was wearing underneath it.

"If I can't talk you into oatmeal, what about some fruit? An English muffin?"

He barely heard the words. "That works for me."

"There are strawberries washed and cut up in the fridge," she said. "I'll put a muffin in the toaster."

"You don't have to feed me," he protested.

"I know. Just my way of saying thanks for putting me up and putting up with me."

"Yeah. You're really hard to take."

"I know. It's a flaw I'm working on."

He wanted to tell her not to change on his account. From where he was standing, she was practically perfect. His flaws on the other hand, were *flaws*. Top of the list was letting people down. His stepbrother for one.

The two of them had bonded over their disapproval when his father married Todd's mother and couldn't have been more different. Nick played football and basketball while cystic fibrosis made Todd frail and sickly. But he was smart and had a sharp wit and keen sense of humor. That made Nick's part in losing him so much worse.

Todd was just home from the hospital and recovering from a lung infection. He said he was fine and Nick should go when the girl he'd been trying to hook up with finally agreed. While alone his brother had trouble breathing. By the time he got help, his heart gave out from the strain. CF got the blame, not Nick. But he would never forgive himself any more than he would lose control of his feelings.

"Here you go."

Ryleigh put a bowl of strawberries and a plate holding a buttered English muffin in front of him. She spooned oatmeal for herself from the pot on the stove, then sat on a stool at the overhanging bar of the island. It took him a moment to pull himself back from the dark thoughts. If she noticed, she didn't say anything.

He took the bar stool beside hers, then bit into the circle of toasted muffin. "Good."

"It's whole wheat." She took a spoonful of her hot cereal and studied him for a reaction.

"Still good."

"And good for you."

He narrowed his gaze on her. "When did you turn into the nutrition police?"

"It was a Wednesday," she said, looking completely serious. "I think it was raining."

"You're mocking me."

"Yes. And it's for your own good. Keeps you humble. Someone needs to remind you you're human."

He was all too aware of that, but had to ask, "Why?"

"Because." She scraped her bowl and ate the last of the cereal. "You're a doctor. A pediatric pulmonologist. By definition you save sick children from serious lung diseases. Grateful parents bow and scrape. Don't get me wrong. What you do is pretty darn awesome. But that kind of reverence day in and day out can tend to make you forget you put your pants on one leg at a time."

His lips twitched, but he managed a serious tone when he asked, "And you've made it your mission to remind me?"

"A dirty job, but someone has to do it."

He noted the arch of her brow, the gleam in her brown eyes, an amused curve to her full lips. This sassy side was new. He liked it.

"You used to have more respect," he said.

For just a second, shadows blocked out the gleam in her eyes. When it disappeared, she tilted her head to the side and sent him a saucy look. "I still do. But now I'm not trying to impress you."

"Clearly." He finished the muffin while admiring looking her over. "But you're trying to make an impression on someone. Nice power suit."

"Thanks." She smoothed a hand over the skirt on her thighs. "I've got a lunch meeting with a local business group to make a pitch for Children's Medical Charities. Keep your fingers crossed."

"They won't be able to resist you, Ry."

He should know. She was the only woman who'd ever made him want to lose control, but years of practice had enabled him to resist the urge to go all in. He'd watched his rock of a father implode after his mother walked out. Nick would never allow himself to feel something so strong that it could fundamentally change him if it was yanked away. He was definitely a product of his formative years. No one would get through his defenses and he wouldn't let down somebody who was counting on him.

With Ryleigh, he'd messed up on both counts. And she was here now, so he could make it up to her.

"I hope you're right." She crossed her middle and index fingers for luck. "Because it takes money to make it. I'm going to hit them up for donations to put on the fundraising gala. Auction items like spa and golf weekends. Hotel getaway packages including fabulous dinners. Art items. But also services for the event itself. Food from celebrity chefs. Flowers. Entertainment. It's the biggest fundraiser of the year and my work on this will be closely watched."

"I can personally vouch for your powers of persuasion. If you can get me to chow down a whole-wheat muffin, you'll have them eating out of your hand."

"We'll see." She slid off the stool and picked up their dirty dishes and silverware. "I'll put these in the dishwasher." Her cell phone beeped just as she turned on the water at the sink. "Can you get that? I hope they haven't cancelled the meeting on me."

Nick picked up her phone and read the text. The words had his body reacting even before the significance of the message got through to his brain. "You're ovulating."

She straightened with a dripping plate in her hand and looked at him. "What?"

"Your ovary is releasing an egg."

"Right this minute? How do you know?"

He held up the phone. "It didn't turn purple or anything but, and I quote, 'Your fertile window opens today and lasts five more days. Stress can get in the way of conception so relax and get a massage, meditate or do yoga.'"

"I guess I should explain." She laughed, but it wasn't sassy and brash like her relaxed amusement while eating breakfast together. Now she was knee-deep in nerves. "In my research, one of the things I found was an alert system. You put in the pertinent personal data and when it's that time, you'll get a text message."

"So, now what?" Blood pounded in his ears and his body was humming like a tuned up Ferrari.

She closed the dishwasher door and stood on the other side of the island, her gaze never leaving his. "Now you help me to have a baby."

"Okay. Tonight will be—"

"Wait. It's Monday. You always get home late. Tomorrow will be okay."

"Carlton can handle things." It was one night. Whether or not Carlton Gallagher worked into the practice, for one or two nights—just hours really—Nick could take the time. "I'll be home."

"You're sure?"

"Absolutely. Unless you changed your mind?" Part of him wished she had. The other part had his fingers crossed.

She shook her head. "I'll be here, too."

He wanted to pump his arm and holler hallelujah. Then reality smacked him like a bug on a windshield. Being her buddy was better than being nothing to her. What if this plan destroyed the friendship?

He had to chance it. The marriage fell apart because of him. He'd disappointed her then and wouldn't do it now, especially after giving his word. Backing out wasn't an option.

So a Monday that started out great now had the potential to end up in awesome territory.

He had a sex date with Ryleigh.

After work, Ryleigh pulled into the driveway. It was nearly seven, but Nick wasn't home yet, which was kind of a relief. She had a chance to catch her breath and calm down. Although why she thought calming down was a possibility was anyone's guess. Her nerves had been on high alert all day because every second that ticked by brought her closer to sex with her ex.

She unlocked the door and walked inside, turning on lights everywhere on her way upstairs to the guest room to change. Nick had complimented her on the red suit, but somehow it didn't seem appropriate. After dropping her purse on the dresser, she slipped off her heels and out of the skirt and jacket before hanging them in the closet. Standing there in her panties and bra, she wondered what to put on. A bolder, braver woman might wait for him naked, but Ryleigh wasn't feeling especially bold or brave.

Maybe some sexy lingerie. Something flirtatious. Except flirting wasn't necessary because they were in agreement about what was going to happen. So that was a bad idea even if she had a qualifying outfit. Which she didn't. There hadn't been a flirtatious or lingerie-worthy man since Nick.

That left her two choices: the frumpy robe over her underwear or a T-shirt and sweatpants. The former would be convenient, but she opted for number two. Practical reasons. Eleven hours had passed since he'd read her ovulation alert and he might have changed his mind. If so, being dressed was far less humiliating.

After pulling a red and white Runnin' Rebels shirt over her head and slipping on a pair of black sweatpants, she checked her hair, brushed her teeth and dabbed perfume behind her ears and on her wrists.

"Break a leg," she said to her reflection in the mirror.

Just as she hit the bottom stair, the front door opened and there was Nick. He had a bouquet of flowers in one hand, a bag and bottle of wine in the other. Just a guess, but it didn't look like he'd changed his mind.

"Hi," she said, heart thumping as she met him in the entryway.

He held out the flowers. "For you."

"Thanks. You really didn't have to."

"I know. It's nothing fancy." He put the pink carnations wrapped in green cellophane in her arms.

Her heart thumped a little harder and she went all gooey

inside. How sweet was this? If only he'd made a single similar gesture when they were married, the marriage might have survived. Leaving had been the hardest thing she'd ever done and one look at Nick reminded her why.

In his old brown leather jacket, cotton shirt and jeans, he couldn't possibly look more dashing, more masculine, more handsome. That attitude and his smile had swept her off her feet before, but this time she was in full control of her heart.

"You're very sweet," she said, burying her nose in the fragrant flowers.

"Remember that when you're poring over project proposals and trying to decide which kids program to fund."

She arched an eyebrow. "So, this is a bribe?"

"Actually I just thought of it. But, all causes being equal, how can you turn down the guy who brought you flowers?"

"I'll take that under advisement." She looked at him and wished she could get a grip on her nerves. Facing down billionaire Las Vegas businessmen hadn't rattled her like this. "Right now I'm going to put these in water. Do you have a vase?"

"Not that I know of." He went to the kitchen cupboard and pulled out a white plastic pitcher from the top shelf, a place way beyond her reach. "How about this?"

"That will work." Grateful to have something to keep her hands busy, she filled it with water, then unwrapped the flowers and put them in. She moved the arrangement to the center of the island and said, "Pretty."

Nick set down the bag and pulled out "to go" boxes. "I stopped at Peretti's for a bottle of wine and appetizers."

She stared at him. This wasn't exactly a recreation of their first date. But sort of. The same food followed by the same physical activity. The difference was that this time she knew exactly what she was doing. Sort of.

Again her heart thumped. He looked so cute, so appealing. The effort he'd made was incredibly sweet, but for reasons she didn't understand, that kicked up her nerves even more, into the reddest of red-alert zones.

What now? Food, wine, bed? Or bed, food, wine? Would they even want to eat afterward? Or would they retire to their respective corners? Should she make the first move? If so, what would that move be?

She leaned a hip against the island and folded her arms over her chest. "How was your day? Was there a lot to do after the weekend? I guess not. Because you're home now. I mean you said you would be, but stuff happens. After all, you're a doctor and if I remember right fall is a busy time for a pediatric pulmonologist. Kids go back to school and share every virus in the universe with friends and family. And allergies kick up triggering asthma. Not to mention sports—"

He touched a finger to her lips, stopping the verbal dump. "Take a breath. If you need it I've got oxygen in the car."

"Really?"

"No." His gaze skipped over her face, studying her intently. Looking for symptoms maybe? For a diagnosis? "You're nervous."

Diagnosis right on. "What gave me away?"

"Aside from your monologue? All of which you remembered correctly, by the way." One corner of his mouth turned up before he was completely serious again. "Are you sure you want to do this?"

"Yes." Then she read between the lines of his question. "Have you changed your mind?"

"I notified my answering service that I'm unavailable

and instructed them to call Dr. Gallagher if there's an emergency." A dark, delicious heat burned in his eyes. "I'll take care of the wine. You handle the appetizers. We'll sit and...just talk."

"Sounds like a plan."

Nick expertly opened the bottle and popped out the cork. While she arranged mozzarella sticks, fried zucchini and calamari on a plate, he carried two glasses of cabernet into the family room and set them on the table. Then he turned on the gas log in the fireplace before making a circuit of the room to shut off most of the lights. It was romantic.

But that was just Nick, she told herself. A goal-oriented overachiever. She was making this way more compli-cated than the situation called for. *That's* what was caus-ing the nerves. She needed to separate feelings from the physical.

Act like a man.

Carrying the plate to the other room she whispered to herself, "Food, wine, talk."

After setting it on the table, she took a glass then settled on the sofa, tucking her legs up beside her. Nick sat on her other side, close enough so that she could feel the warmth from his body. At some point he'd taken his jacket off, but the cotton shirt was an effectively manly look, too.

"So," she said, taking a generous sip of wine. "How was your day, really?"

"Busy. And for all the reasons you mentioned." He laughed. "Kids do get sick this time of year. They're play-ing soccer and football. There's pollen and dust. Not to mention smoke coming into the valley from the wildfires in California. That kicks up all kinds of respiratory dis-tress in kids."

Ryleigh drank her wine as he talked. Concern for

children showed in his eyes and she'd had firsthand experience with his dedication. When he got a call about a child in crisis, he was always available. "It's a good thing you've got Dr. Gallagher to take some of the load off."

"If he works out. That's not a done deal yet."

"But he's a good doctor." It wasn't a question. Nick wouldn't have instructed his service that he wasn't available if there was no trust in the other man.

"He'll do."

Nick got up and went to the kitchen, bringing back the wine bottle to fill her glass. He took a cheese stick from the plate, then sat beside her, this time close enough that their thighs brushed. Her breathing kicked up a notch, especially when the scent of his skin filled her head.

"Now tell me about your day. Did you get the businesses to cough stuff up till they screamed and cried uncle?" He took a bite of the appetizer.

She laughed. "The meeting went well. They were very generous. Most were familiar with the work Children's Medical Charities does."

As she talked and drank her wine, relaxation kicked in. The fire, but mostly the man, made her feel warm all over. "I think everything is going to come together nicely."

That's when Nick cupped her cheek in his palm and kissed her.

Chapter Five

The sudden move shocked Ryleigh speechless, which wasn't much of a problem really since her mouth was otherwise occupied in a really spectacular way. Nick moved his lips over hers, slow and sweet, then trailed nibbling kisses down her chin and across her jaw. There was a place just behind her ear that was especially sensitive and he sucked on it. A feeling like an electric shock shot into her breasts and down her legs. She heard his breathing—fast, harsh, ragged.

He stopped, not touching her anywhere except his breath on her cheek. "You smell good."

"Thanks." She squeezed the wineglass hard, fully expecting it to shatter, then rested her forehead on his shoulder. "So do you."

"Good to know."

"So, what was that? Sneak attack?"

"If you say so." There was humor in his voice and a

sexy note of need. "Call it an icebreaker. To get rid of the nerves. It's not a massage or meditation. But I thought it might help."

"You thought right." It was hard for her to stay nervous when desire ripped through her like a tornado in Kansas farm country. "It was nice."

"There's more where that came from. Are you ready?"

She nodded, unable to form a word what with need knotting in her throat.

Nick took her wineglass and set it on the table along with his own. "This is the last time I'm going to ask. You haven't changed your mind, have you?"

"No." The fact that she really, *really* wanted him was just an unexpected bonus in her quest to get pregnant.

"Okay." He stood, then reached a hand down to her.

She put her fingers into his wide, warm palm and let him pull her to her feet. "Okay."

Wrapping her hand in his, Nick led her to the stairs and they climbed together. It was like so many other times, except now there was no marriage. That didn't really matter. She'd yearned for him before they tied the knot and for a long time after the divorce. The way her body quivered and burned for him now proved that she didn't need to be in love to get physical.

At the top of the stairs, he turned right into the master bedroom and hit the switch just inside the door. Instantly a bedside lamp turned on. Like too many times to count, Nick walked to the side of the bed closest to the french doors leading to the outside balcony. The shades were drawn and white shutters closed on all the windows, sealing them in a private world for two.

He put a hand on the comforter and she did the same on her side, letting muscle memory take over. As they worked together folding down the bedding, she couldn't tear her gaze away from his. Intensity flared, turning his eyes to blue flames. When the sheets were uncovered, Nick pulled his shirt from the waistband of his jeans and undid the first button.

Ryleigh's mouth went dry. Slowly he unfastened each one, parting the cotton and revealing teasing glimpses of the hair-dusted chest beneath. Her heart was pounding when his shirt finally hung open. She held her breath, waiting for him to take it off. To her extreme disappointment, he didn't.

"Have you done any more research that I should know about?" His voice was deep and rough and sexy.

"On?" Along with the rest of her body, her brain was having a meltdown. One word was all she could manage.

"The best position to achieve conception."

She shook her head. "I've looked extensively. As I told you, there are two schools of thought and—"

"No definitive study exists for proof of either." His grin revealed straight white teeth.

Her legs went weak and a trembling started in her thighs. "Each side makes a valid point in supporting their theory."

He walked around the bed and stopped in front of her, threading the fingers of both hands through the hair around her face. "Then, let's do our own study."

"We'll write a paper."

"Or something."

Gently, he held her face in his hands. In what felt like slow motion, he lowered his head until his lips brushed hers. The touch was tender and chaste. There was nothing insistent in the way he took her mouth over and over, letting familiar sensations drift through her. She slid her hands inside his opened shirt and settled her palms at his waist. The skin was too hot, too tempting and she explored the expanse of his back, feeling the play of muscles rippling there. Emotions washed over her that she remembered from another lifetime but could have been just yesterday.

She wanted him just like before.

He moved a hand from her face and placed it on her lower back, just above her butt, urging her closer to his solid strength. They were pressed together from chest to knee and she could feel his need.

Just like before.

Knowing he still wanted her unleashed a flood of pent-up passion, and she kissed him back, putting all the frustration from the last two years into it. Her body was so in sync with his that she felt the instant when gentleness turned fierce and tender gave way to wild.

His breathing went from slightly rasping to ragged and harsh. His hands moved urgently over her, restless and demanding. With her palms pressed flat on his back, she could feel his increasing tension.

The marriage might be dead, but attraction and desire were not. Position planning and pregnancy strategy were forgotten as their bodies remembered the way it used to be between them.

Ryleigh rubbed her fingers over the dusting of hair on his chest until her nerve endings tingled. She touched his nipple and felt it grow hard as he hissed out a breath.

"That's not playing fair."

She looked up and smiled. "I never agreed to."

"Okay, but just remember you started it—" A challenging expression slid into his eyes, one that said he intended to finish it. He gripped the hem of her T-shirt and tugged it up and off, tossed it over his shoulder, then pulled her against him again.

She felt his fingers on her back just before the sides of her bra parted. When she settled her hand on the zipper of his jeans, he groaned. The tempo of passion shot up another notch as a silent signal passed between them. He pushed at her sweatpants while she struggled with his belt and jeans. When they were finally naked, he lowered her to the mattress and settled on his side next to her.

He took her breast in his hand and brushed his thumb over the taut nipple, sending exquisite electricity arcing through her. As his hand trailed over her belly and down between her legs, her breath came in gasps, as if she couldn't draw enough air into her lungs. Her hips moved, instinctively working to contain and increase the pleasure of his touch.

He slid a finger into her and tension coiled between her legs and her thighs trembled. With his mouth on hers, he swallowed her needy moan. He bent over her a little more and she lifted her hips, letting him know without words what she wanted. Needed. She felt him smile and knew he knew, but continued to tease her with his hands, fingers and mouth.

Tension and longing coiled and grew until she shattered into a million points of light. He held her while she came back together and the tremors slowed. Then he levered himself over her and nudged her legs wider. The feel of him pushing inside started the pleasure growing yet again. He reached between them to rub the nub of nerve endings as he stroked inside her, pushing her again to the breaking point.

His breathing grew harsh and ragged, while intensity flashed in his eyes. Then he groaned and went still before burying his face in the crook of her neck. She felt her own release break free and trembles of sensation flooded through her again.

Ryleigh wasn't sure how long he held her and wasn't quite ready when he let her go.

After rolling onto his back he said, "Wow."

"Wow, indeed." She blew out a long breath.

A few moments later he lifted onto his elbow and looked down at her. "I have it on good authority that remaining in a prone position can't hurt the chances of conception."

"Ah," she said smiling, "A man who listens and remembers. You're a phenomenon, Doctor."

"I can do better than that." He kissed her forehead, then pulled a pair of sweatpants from a drawer and stepped into them. "Stay here, I'll be right back. And don't forget to relax."

Ryleigh laughed as he pulled the sheet and blanket over her. She probably couldn't move even if the house was on fire. Her whole body felt lax and bursting with satisfaction. But now that she'd caught her breath, the wonder of it all sank in.

She and Nick might have just made a baby.

But there was no she and Nick. They weren't a couple who could bask in the glow and excitement of starting this journey, anticipating together this next chapter in their life. That made her a little sad, but it couldn't be helped. As usual, everything in life was a trade-off. To get what she wanted more than anything, she had to feel this feeling of regret.

Nick reappeared with the wine bottle and two glasses, which he set on the nightstand beside her. "I brought you something."

"That's really sweet."

"I'm a sweet guy."

"Yes, you are," she agreed.

But it got better. He plumped the pillows behind her until she was half sitting. Then he poured and handed her the glass of wine, took one for himself and settled on the bed beside her. It wasn't exactly like post coitus cuddling, she thought. And there was no reason to expect it. That would be personal. This was nothing more than biology.

"What should we drink to?" he asked.

She thought for a moment, then said, "The future. May we both get what we want."

"That sounds like a plan," he said, touching his glass to hers. "I hope all your dreams come true."

The words tugged at her heart. Then she realized that this wasn't like before. The realization jolted her, left her shaken. The experience, the sex, had never felt quite so powerful and it wasn't just about trying to make a baby.

This was different because she had Nick's full attention. She didn't think that had ever happened when they were married. At least not that she could remember. It was probably just a fluke, an aberration, but testing the theory was loaded with risk.

They were friends and she wanted to keep it that way. Too many nights like this had the potential to coax her to the dark side. With luck, tonight had produced a baby. If so, she and Nick wouldn't have to see each other except for chance meetings at the hospital.

She crossed her fingers and tried to relax, let Nick's "guys" do their thing. She hoped the first time was the charm because doing this again could be problematic for their beautiful friendship.

On Saturday morning Nick closed and locked the front door, then followed Ryleigh to his SUV. After getting in, he turned the key in the ignition and drove out of the development on the way to Mercy Medical Center.

He couldn't say he looked forward to the children's asthma clinic every month, but this time Ryleigh was going with him. That alone didn't explain his excellent good spirits, but if he was being honest with himself, that was part of it. The other part was sex on alternating nights since her fertile window opened. She'd informed him that doing the deed *every* night could deplete sperm count.

He'd been willing to take the chance that he had enough guys on the in-between nights to achieve the objective for which he'd been recruited. Apparently Ryleigh didn't agree. Or she had other reasons for working late every other evening, which was probably for the best. As much as he felt in control, reminders that this was only an arrangement were a good thing. And he tried not to think about what would happen if she got pregnant.

Or if she didn't.

Would she go to someone else to get the job done? The thought pissed him off.

"Nick?"

"What?" He glanced over at her in the passenger seat.

"Is something wrong?"

"No. Why?"

She was clutching the overhead handle on her side of the car. "You're going a little fast."

The speedometer told him she was right, and he eased off the accelerator. "Sorry. Things on my mind."

His rational side kicked in and he figured if she didn't get pregnant she'd probably get checked out to make sure there wasn't a physical problem preventing conception. He would do the same. And if he was the problem, he'd... There was no point in borrowing trouble, although it was hard for him not to. After losing Todd sooner than anyone expected, he'd learned to brace himself for the worst so when it happened he was prepared.

Ryleigh glanced over at him as he pulled onto the 215

Beltway. "So how many kids usually show up at these clinics?"

"It varies. A few to standing room only. Sometimes parents come alone, just for information." He merged into traffic, then briefly met her gaze. "I've adjusted things since we first started doing it."

"Who's 'we'?"

"Myself. The respiratory therapy staff from Mercy Medical."

"Are they volunteering their time?" She was jotting things down on a notepad in her lap.

"The director is. Tom's a salaried employee, but he shows up to help the women's group set up the equipment and make sure a respiratory staff member is there to do the lung-volume screenings on the kids. The therapist is paid an hourly rate for the time."

"What's a lung volume?" She tapped her pen on the pad.

"We have the kids blow into a peak flow meter to register the fastest flow rate of air on exhalation. If they don't reach target, it means airways are starting to shut down and intervention is needed, usually a rescue inhaler. If that doesn't work, the kid probably needs to go to the E.R."

And speaking of air, the inside of this car hadn't smelled so good since... Come to think of it, probably not since the last time Ryleigh had ridden in it. Long after her fragrance had faded, he'd sworn he could still smell her. In the house, too. Eventually he'd gotten the message that he was alone.

But not lately. Having her around had been too nice, along with knowing he wasn't going home to an empty house. But when she left—and she would—he'd go through the alone process again and be fine. There was no doubt in his mind, because he'd gotten very good at keeping his feelings under control. He never let himself stray past the point of no return.

"So what adjustments have you made?" Her voice, a low husky sound that was firmly in the sexy range, snapped him to attention.

"What?"

"You mentioned adjustments to the asthma clinic presentation. What are they?"

"Oh." He needed to focus. "Now I make general remarks about what asthma is, things that trigger an episode and what to do if there is one."

"All good information."

"I think this clinic is in the McDonald meeting room." He looked over and she nodded. "So there should be handouts and bullet points projected onto a screen so anyone who wants to can follow along. Then I see the kids and their parents individually, to answer one-on-one questions."

"Okay." She flipped the notepad closed, then put it in her purse.

"So you're crashing my party to do a report?"

She nodded. "CMC funds the project. It's my job to make sure the money is well spent. Since you're busier in the office, do you expect a good turnout for the clinic?"

"Yeah. This is traditionally a tough time of year for kids and adults with breathing problems. And the women's group does a good job of advertising the event."

From Mercy Medical Center Parkway, he made a left turn into the parking lot, then found a space close to the front of the hospital. When they walked near enough to the entrance, the automatic double doors whispered open. Inside, their feet echoed on the marble tiles. Skylights above let lots of sunshine into the lobby. After turning to the left, they moved down the corridor until a tripod stand with a placard announcing the asthma clinic told them this was the right place.

A young woman with dark hair sat behind a table just in front of the door. "Hi, Dr. Damian."

"Good to see you, Laura." He put his hand at Ryleigh's waist and resisted the urge to pull her closer to his side. "This is Ryleigh Evans. She's the regional coordinator for Children's Medical Charities."

"It's nice to meet you."

Ryleigh smiled. "Same here. You do good work."

"We couldn't do what we do without the volunteers," Nick explained. "It's Laura's responsibility to sign people in and make sure they fill out paperwork with basic medical information. Later the kids' test results will be put into the hospital computer system so that if they come in to the E.R., we have a starting point. That speeds up the treatment process."

"Sounds like a terrific program," Ryleigh commented.

"I think they're ready for you, Doctor," Laura said.

In the large room, rows of folding chairs were set up on one side, while the other had three tables for one-on-one consultation. At each station there was a laptop computer staffed by a respiratory therapist to do spirometry. They had a child blow into the tube and it measured lung capacity, how much air was being moved in and out. If the residual volume of air in the lungs increased, it meant airways were obstructed. Other respiratory therapists were showing the kids how to get the best results from peak flow meters that each child could take home.

He looked down at Ryleigh. "I'm going to do my thing."

"I'll just wander around and observe."

Nick nodded, then walked over to the lecture area.

"Hello, thanks for coming today. I'm Doctor Nick Damian, a pediatric pulmonologist. I work with infants and children up to eighteen years old who have diagnosed lung diseases. But today we're focusing specifically on asthma."

He'd given this talk so many times he could practically do it in his sleep. First there were pictures of a normal airway and one constricted, closing off air flow. Then he covered the most common asthma attack triggers—pollen, a cold or flu virus, exercise.

Finally he stressed the need to understand that there were excellent treatments and medications available and new, better ones coming on the market all the time. Years ago the best meds made patients shaky and caused the heart to race. These days therapy was much improved.

If Todd had lived, if he, Nick, hadn't screwed up and left him alone, there would be new therapies and drugs to prolong his life. CF patients were living longer now and where there was life, there was hope.

But Todd had neither and Nick would never forgive himself for that. All he could do now was be there for the patients who needed him. He wouldn't let anyone down again.

His gaze automatically found Ryleigh sitting in the back row. He felt the heavy weight of responsibility for the failure of their marriage and was doing everything he could to make it up to her. Did he still get absolution for that sin when he was enjoying the hell out of making love to her?

But that wasn't something to be asked or answered here. He looked at the concerned parents in front of him. "I'd be happy to take questions now."

He spent the next ten minutes doing that, then announced that he would be evaluating the breath-screening results. When he'd talked to everyone, easing fears, offering his informed medical opinion, he shook hands with the respiratory therapy volunteers. One of them was Harlow Marcelli, a green-eyed brunette he often saw in the Pediatric Intensive Care Unit.

"Great job today, Marcelli," he said.

"Thanks, Doc." She closed the laptop. "When are you going to dump this Saturday gig for a day on the golf course?"

"For one thing, and this is pretty important, I don't play golf."

She laughed. "But you must have something better to do."

The first thing that popped into his mind was Ryleigh. He liked hanging with her, but that wasn't for public consumption. "Not really."

While he was chatting, Ryleigh came up behind him. Her perfume set his senses on stun.

"Nick?"

When he turned, he saw that she wasn't alone. She stood there with a young boy and a woman who was probably his mom.

"This is Marilyn and her son, David Negri."

"Nice to meet you." Nick shook their hands. "How did you hear about the clinic?"

The sandy-haired, blue-eyed kid looked intense. "There were flyers at school and I talked my mom into bringing me."

"How old are you?"

"Thirteen. I'm in eighth grade."

"Are you planning to go out for football next year?" he asked. "You're big enough."

"I'd like to right now. There are leagues going on right now, but my mom won't let me." The kid sent her a look filled with teenage angst and testosterone-fueled hostility. "She's afraid my asthma will flare up."

"For good reason." The plump brunette in her late thirties looked anxiously up at the boy. "He talked me into letting him try soccer and ended up in the E.R. because he was having trouble breathing. Scared me to death. And he can't understand that it's something a parent never wants to go through again. Especially a single mom."

"I understand," Nick said. "But there are ways to manage the disease so that doesn't happen."

"Like what?" she asked.

"Using appropriate medications before exercise. Possibly an inhaler."

David frowned. "Isn't that the tube thing you suck on?" When Nick nodded, he said, "Do I have to?"

"If you want to play." Nick had a feeling he knew where this was going.

"All my friends will make fun of me."

"Then they're not really your friends. And if being responsible with your medications makes you a wimp, then join the club. There are a lot of pro athletes who are asthmatic. They do what's necessary in order to play the game they love."

"What does the inhaler do?" his mother asked.

"It opens up the airways and prevents an attack. If one happens, there are rescue medications to keep it in check. My job is to help manage the disease and not just while David is a kid. It's about preventing permanent lung damage that can affect him when he's an adult."

Marilyn didn't look convinced. "Do you have children, Doctor?"

"No." He met Ryleigh's gaze and wondered what she was thinking.

"If you did," the woman persisted, "and he or she was asthmatic, would you let him, or her, play sports?"

"I would." He'd answered this question countless times before without any emotional connection to his answer. For him it was just the medical facts because he'd never been a parent. He looked at Ryleigh's flat stomach and realized she could be pregnant right now. It took effort, but he pulled himself back to the topic. "With the proper protocols in place there's no reason to eliminate exercise from a healthy lifestyle."

"See, Mom?" the kid said. "You gotta let me sign up. If I don't, next year in high school everyone will know more than me. Besides, Eric's doing it."

"If Eric jumped off the stratosphere would you follow?" Nick asked.

"I know what you're saying," David told him. "And I don't want to play football just because he is. I just want to play. I've always wanted to, since I was a kid."

Nick wanted to laugh, but held back. This kid was still a kid. "If it's what you want, you should go for it." The boy started to pump his arm in celebration, but Nick held up a finger. "But you need to get a physical. Talk to your primary care doctor about it."

"Do you have a card?" Marilyn asked him.

Nick hesitated. "I'm here to educate parents about asthma."

The woman nodded. "You wouldn't be stealing a patient. I've been wanting to change doctors. David's pediatrician is a woman, Dr. Schwartz."

"She's very good."

"I agree. When he was a little boy. But now…" She looked up at the son who was taller then her.

Nick reached over to the table beside him and grabbed

a handout. "This information sheet has my office number at the top."

"So you're going to let me play, Mom?" the kid asked hopefully.

"I think so." She held up a finger in warning. "Providing you get Dr. Damian's approval."

David smiled for the first time since walking up. "Thanks."

"Don't thank me. You got the flyer at school and brought your mom here. You made it happen, pal."

The kid beamed. "It would be cool if you came to a game."

Nick didn't know what to say. Patients needed his medical skills, not his friendship. But there was something about this kid. It was a good feeling to be part of helping him achieve his dream.

"That would be cool," he finally said.

Marilyn hesitated when her son walked over to the refreshment table for a cookie. She smiled at Ryleigh. "Thank you for introducing us."

"I didn't do anything. It was just so obvious from what David said that he wanted to play." Ryleigh shrugged. "It does my heart good to see him so happy."

"Me, too." She looked up at Nick and grinned. "You'll make a terrific father some day."

Nick stared at Ryleigh's back as she walked away. She could be carrying his baby right now. That would, biologically speaking, make him a father. He'd known, intellectually, but the whole thing became more real somehow. Emotions kicked in, feelings a lot like wanting and needing. Yearning was there, too. He needed to sort them out and push them away.

If he didn't, there would be hell to pay.

Chapter Six

It was Saturday night and Ryleigh was alone.

Until temporarily moving in with Nick she'd spent most Saturday nights alone, but tonight felt worse somehow. While fixing herself a salad she tried to fix the oh-poor-me mood. Maybe it had been triggered by the brooding look on Nick's face after the asthma clinic. He'd brought her home, then said he had some things to do. He'd been gone ever since and she couldn't help wondering. They weren't married; she had no claim on his time. Except…

He'd gone quiet and intense right after that grateful mom had said he would be a good father. The thing is, the woman was right. Ryleigh had always felt the same way, but he hadn't loved her enough to make the effort. His guilt over that was the only reason he'd agreed to try and give her a baby now, but he would keep himself distant. That made her sad and she needed to get over it. Nick Damian hadn't changed. He was still the same man who'd swept her off her feet, then disappeared.

"Not unlike today," she said to herself.

After chopping salad, tomato, avocado and cucumber with a little more enthusiasm than was probably necessary, she cut up a cooked chicken breast and mixed oil and vinegar into everything. Then she sat at the island with the bowl and looked at the real estate section of the newspaper, spreading the pages out in front of her. The front door opened and closed, prompting her pulse to pound and her heart to hammer. She was really annoyed that he could make that happen just by walking in the damn house.

She figured he'd appear in the kitchen any second and she was right. Annoyance was no defense against his dark, wavy hair, deep blue eyes and the sexy scruff on his jaw. Her pulse and heart continued to do their own thing despite the animosity she waved around to keep them in line.

"Hi." Nick walked to the refrigerator and pulled out a bottle of water. He looked tired.

Not her problem. Yet that didn't stop her from wanting to know where he'd been, what he'd been doing. Except it was a need-to-know basis and his comings and goings weren't something she needed to know.

"Hi." She finished chewing a bite of salad. "If I'd known you'd be here for dinner, I'd have made a bigger salad."

After a long drink from the water bottle, he looked at her. "I already ate."

"Good." She didn't need to feel guilty for just thinking about herself. It wasn't one of her finest qualities but had definitely been on overdrive during her marriage. She was working on the flaw. "So, the asthma clinic had a really good turnout."

"Yeah."

"It seems like the kind of project Children's Medical Charities needs to continue funding."

"Good to know."

"With another doctor, we could open it up to more people. Do you think Dr. Gallagher would be interested in helping out?"

"He may not be around."

She hadn't gotten much out of him in the car afterward, and it appeared that wasn't going to change. "Then I'll look into getting someone else."

"What are you reading?" He leaned his forearms on the island's granite countertop and angled his jaw toward the newspaper spread in front of her.

She didn't miss that he'd abruptly changed the subject, but let it go. "Real estate section."

"Ah."

"I was wondering if you remember the name of the agent we used to buy this house." Ryleigh had really connected with the woman who had picked out properties for them to look at that were all wonderful. "I really liked her."

"Her card is in my desk. Are you thinking about looking for something?"

Her mouth was full of salad and chicken, preventing her from instantly answering. That gave her a chance to study his expression. For all the good it did. She couldn't tell if the intensity spike was disapproval or residual brooding.

After swallowing, she said, "I'm thinking about getting a place of my own. The apartment is pretty awful and I can't stay here indefinitely. I need a house, either to rent or buy."

"Buy," he said. "Definitely."

She poked a cucumber with her fork. "Why definitely?"

"It's a tax write-off and renting makes you vulnerable to the landlord/owner. If the place is sold out from under you, moving could be inconvenient." He thought for a moment. "Also, you don't know whether or not the mortgage gets paid. If it doesn't, and is foreclosed, you could be out a lot of money."

"How so?"

"When you rent, up-front money is usually first and last month and security deposit. Chances are if they're behind on payments, you could be evicted by the bank and the owner has no money to reimburse you for anything."

"Good point. I didn't think about that."

"Times are tough. It's happening a lot here right now."

"How sad to think about people losing their homes."

"Yeah. There are things you can do to protect yourself, but buying outright puts all the control in your hands." He twisted the white cap back onto the water bottle. "There may be first-time buyer incentives from mortgage companies. And interest rates are really low right now. Also there's a lot of inventory. It's unquestionably a buyer's market. I can help if you need the down payment—"

"No." She wouldn't take anything from him now any more than she did when they divorced. At the time it hadn't felt right and eventually she'd realized half the blame belonged to her, so why should he pay? Besides, money couldn't buy happiness. "I have it."

"Good."

"I'm convinced. Being a homeowner is the way for me to go." She tilted her head. "I think you missed your calling, Nick."

He walked around the island, dropping his empty plastic water bottle in the recycle trash. When he took the stool beside hers, the masculine smell of his skin wrapped around her. Her stomach did that funny little slip and slide, making her want to snuggle against him. But that wasn't part of their bargain.

The only reason for physical contact was to make a baby and her fertility window had closed. Soon she would do a pregnancy test, to find out if there *was* a baby. Until then, except for the fact that she really liked it, there was no reason to be in his arms.

"Missed my calling?" he asked.

"Maybe you should have gone into real estate. Buying and selling property seems up your alley—no pun intended."

He smiled and shook his head. "Not for me. Too much pressure."

"And helping a child who's having difficulty breathing isn't full of stress?"

"That's different."

"What makes it different?" When he stared at her, she added, "Although I think you'd be successful at anything you tried, you've really got a flair for the medical profession."

"What makes you say that?"

"For one thing, you're a legend at Mercy Medical Center." She remembered their first face-to-face meeting in her office after she'd started her job. It wasn't easy to meet a legend on his turf.

"Legend?" One corner of his mouth quirked up as a teasing look slid into his eyes. "That really makes me feel old. I don't think I've reached the minimum age requirement for legend status."

"That condition is waived when everyone talks about you in reverent whispers and awed tones."

"Oh, please—"

"Seriously," she protested. "When I was going through

the interview process for my job, the board of directors spoke about you as if·you had wings, a halo and walked on water. And before you ask, that doesn't mean I'll authorize the necessary funds for ECMO."

"When they interviewed you, did the powers that be know we were divorced?" he asked wryly.

· "I figured it was best to keep that to myself."

He nodded proudly. "Smart."

"Takes one to know one. But there's more to being a good doctor than brains." She'd seen him today with the kids. His dedication was as vivid as his blue eyes. He truly cared about their health. It was more than dealing with one medical crisis after another. Their whole lives and the quality of them was important to him. "So, why did you become a doctor, instead of, say, a real estate agent?"

He shrugged. "I'm good in science and math. Seemed like a good fit."

"With those skills you could have gone into teaching. Engineering. Almost anything. But you didn't. It's more than that."

"It's just a job."

She'd heard all this before and let him get away without answering the question. Not this time. "To do what you do is a special calling, separate from the other qualifications you have. I'd really like to know what made you want to be a doctor, Nick. And before you come up with something witty to distract me, you should know that it's not going to work. I'm prepared to sit here until I get what I want."

"Really?"

"Absolutely." She pushed her empty salad bowl away, then folded her arms over her chest and gave him her very best I-can-wear-you-down look.

It took several moments for him to surrender, but finally he nodded. "You know I had a stepbrother."

"Yes. Todd."

"Yeah." The dark, brooding expression was back. "We were complete opposites. He was sickly, I was an athlete. All we had in common was that neither of us was very happy about our folks getting married."

"But?" she pushed.

"Somehow we bonded. Probably because of a shared hostility toward the parents. He was funny and smart. He called me on my crap and became the little brother I'd never had."

"You still miss him." Ryleigh wasn't asking. His eyes said it all. "How did he die?"

"Todd had cystic fibrosis."

"Obviously I've heard of it, but I don't know much about the disease," she said.

"Most patients are diagnosed by age two. It's caused by a defective gene and its protein product causes the body to produce unusually thick, sticky mucus. It clogs the lungs and leads to life-threatening infections. Todd's life expectancy was always a question mark, but no one figured he would die so young. In the last twenty years, therapies and medications have prolonged patient's lives by years—possibly indefinitely. If he'd survived, there's no telling…"

She'd known his brother died, but Nick would never talk about what happened. Now she knew, but Nick was still holding back. The dark intensity on his face was a giveaway.

Without consciously intending to, she reached over and put her hand on his. She could almost feel how much he wanted to turn it over, palm up, and swallow her fingers in his. "What is it, Nick? There's more, isn't there? Talk to me."

He shook his head, then stood up and backed away,

letting her hand fall to the cold granite. "I'll get you that real estate agent's card."

Before she could stop him, he was gone. She tried not to take it personally. After all, their deal was to check anything personal at the door, but she couldn't quite manage it. Maybe tomorrow.

Right now Nick was her friend and she felt for his pain, wanted to do something to help. She remembered the way parents had looked at him, as if he were a god with all the answers. But he was just a man, a smart and handsome one without a doubt. Still, he had flaws and frailties just like everyone else.

And the worst part of realizing that was it made her like him even more.

The next day Nick followed Ryleigh through a house for sale while the real estate agent waited outside. Some of the things they'd liked about Shelley Peck were her efficiency and sensitivity. She showed them around, pointed out the pros and cons, then disappeared to let them discuss the pros and cons amongst themselves.

He glanced out the living room window and saw the agent in her Lexus SUV. "I was a little surprised you made an appointment to look at houses today. Seems kind of fast."

"Someone cancelled an appointment with Shelley, so I took it." Ryleigh glanced at the room's twelve-foot ceiling and crown molding.

"That's not what I meant. I just didn't think you were in such a rush."

"And whose fault is that?" The glance she slid him was full of irony. "Your financial logic was flawless. There's no reason to wait. Might as well buy something. Get out of your hair. Get settled. In case…"

In case she was pregnant. Thinking about her pregnant made him remember trying to get her that way. That made him want her now which seemed weird. Although anything and nothing made him want her—anytime, anywhere. He pushed the feeling away. No point in borrowing another complication when he had so many to choose from already.

"What do you think of this house?" she asked.

The two-story was about twenty-six hundred square feet with four bedrooms and three baths. Lots of granite in the kitchen, wood floors. It was functional and charming.

"There's no security system," he pointed out.

"Not a deal breaker."

"It is in my opinion." Because he felt protective of her. Always had and probably always would.

"It's pre-wired for a system and I could have one installed. If I loved everything about the place."

"Do you?" he asked.

"I'm not sure. Although the high ceilings are nice and that molding is wonderful."

Nick glanced up. "Too high. That will make the place harder to heat and air condition. The energy bills will be, pardon the pun, through the roof."

Her merry laugh burrowed inside him and brightened the dark corners of his soul. "That's a good point. Let's go see the next one."

They left the house and Shelley took care of putting the key back in the lock box. She looked to be somewhere in her forties, a trim, blue-eyed blonde with shoulder-length hair.

She got in the driver's seat and glanced at Ryleigh beside her in the front, then back at him. "What did you think?"

"It's nice," Ryleigh said. "But I didn't love it."

"I could tell." Shelley started the car. "The next one isn't far from The District and Green Valley Ranch Resort. That makes movies, shopping and really good restaurants close."

During the drive they were quiet, just taking in the greenbelts and walkways through the family-centered neighborhood. Right off Valle Verde Parkway she stopped in front of another two-story house with a small front yard landscaped with desert plants and decorative rock.

Shelley looked at the information sheet. "This is supposed to be in nice condition, lots of extras. It's a little over the price range you gave me."

Nick released his seat belt and leaned forward. "Not a problem if she likes it."

Ryleigh gave him an independent look that was new and very hot, as in sexy hot. "If I like it, I'll handle the cost."

"Everything is negotiable," Shelley told them. "Let's not get ahead of ourselves."

The owners weren't home, so the same routine applied. When the agent left them, Nick stood beside her in the kitchen/family room combination. This property had five bedrooms, including one on the first floor with its own bath.

"What do you think?" she asked.

"The carpet is pretty worn."

"Shelley said the sellers are motivated and offering an allowance. They'll even let the buyer pick out something and have it installed before move-in."

"The floor plan is a little choppy," he added, studying the backyard. "It has a pool."

"I know." She grabbed his arm in her excitement. "Isn't that great?"

"There's no fence." Her hand was still warm as it

gripped his long-sleeved shirt, but he felt the enthusiasm drain out of her. Explaining his motivation for the comment would probably be good. "A small child could wander outside and fall in."

She nodded, but a frown settled in her eyes. "Doesn't look like it would be problematic or costly to add one."

"If you like this house." He studied her face. One part of him hoped she loved the place and would move in tomorrow. Another part hoped she hated it and would stay with him just a little longer. Part two needed some serious therapy.

"I like this house a lot," she said, glancing around. "But there are still more to see."

He nodded. "At least you narrowed the search by price range and square footage. Nothing farther than ten miles from Mercy Medical Center or smaller than twenty-three hundred square feet."

"And still there are so many properties for sale."

"Yeah. Let's go see them."

When they got to the last house on the list, Nick could tell by the look on Ryleigh's face that she liked it a lot. As usual he held his emotions back, but Ryleigh didn't. She'd worn the very same bright-eyed expression when walking through the house they'd bought together.

One of the things he'd always liked about her was that you never had to guess how she was feeling. Happy, sad, grumpy or puzzled, her face showed everything. Right now it was showing unqualified approval.

Shelley didn't miss it, either. "I think this might be the one. You two talk. I'll go sit in the car and make some calls."

When the front door closed, Nick asked, "Is she right?"

"I really like this one," she confirmed. "Love the tile.

It's something I would have picked and goes with the light beige walls."

He leaned a shoulder beside the French doors leading to the rear yard. "You don't think that makes it too dark?"

She shook her head. "The white ceiling not only makes it look higher, but it brightens the room, too."

"The pool takes up most of the backyard."

"It's fenced," she pointed out.

"But that doesn't leave much grass for a kid to play in."

"There's some off to the right. And the private park and play area is across the street."

"You don't think it might get noisy?"

"No." She listened. "It didn't seem like there's much traffic, just people in the neighborhood." She looked around the family room that adjoined the kitchen. "This is the only house we've seen with a fireplace."

"This is Las Vegas. It's not like you need one to stay warm." But he remembered lighting his fireplace to set a romantic mood for sex, and that went under the heading of no good deed goes unpunished.

"But can't you just see it decorated with lighted garland at Christmas?"

"Not really." He was picturing his house without her in it and the emptiness when she was gone.

"That's because you have no whimsy."

He grinned. "I can live without it."

"Not me. And the master bedroom had a ton of it. Big and bright. Didn't you love that Jacuzzi tub?"

Not after he got a vision of being in it with her. Naked. "The closet is too big."

"On what planet?" She looked at him as if aliens were popping out of his chest. "There's no such thing as a closet that's too big."

"If you say so."

"I'm not alone. Ninety-nine-point-nine percent of women would say the same thing." She tilted her head and studied him, a frown lurking in her big brown eyes. "What's with you today, Nick?"

"Nothing." Denial was as good a place to hide as anywhere else. "Why do you ask?"

"Because you weren't this much trouble when we bought a house together."

"That's because I just let you pick it out."

He remembered as if it were yesterday. When the idea of house hunting came up, they'd just been married. He'd have bought her the moon to make her happy.

And she was. For a while. Then he left her alone too much, more than he needed to. At least she didn't turn to another man. Her leaving was hard, but he didn't think he could take that.

Backlit by the French doors, she rested her hands on her hips. "The thing is, this time you don't get a vote."

"Did you not say that you wanted my opinion?"

"Yes. But not if all you see is negative. I'm picking it out and making the final decision."

And there was the source of his conflict. He wanted her under his roof every bit as much as he didn't want her there. He'd thought it would be no big deal, but he hadn't counted on the scent of her skin and the sound of her voice surrounding him.

He hadn't anticipated that her essence, her presence, would remind him every second of every day what he would never get back. Even if he wanted to, there was no point in trying because he'd only disappoint her again. And he'd sworn never to do that.

He'd once heard his father say that his mother was as necessary to him as breathing. When she left, he never recovered and remarrying was a mistake. His dad was a broken man and nothing could fix him, not even a second marriage. It was very possible he'd died of a broken heart. Nick wouldn't be a chip off the old block. He couldn't let himself need anyone or be lost without them. Ryleigh had come awfully close to doing that to him, but he'd gotten over it.

When he'd invited her to live with him this time, it never crossed his mind that he'd be so completely tempted to let go of his control with her. Taking a step back was what he needed to do.

"You're right." Nick met her gaze. "You should make an offer on this house."

Chapter Seven

Nick wasn't liking this Monday nearly as much as the last one. He hadn't seen Ryleigh that morning, for coffee, breakfast or anything else. Although it didn't stop him, he had no business thinking about sex. Her fertile window had slammed shut several days ago.

As if that wasn't enough to justify his foul mood, he'd made a complete ass of himself during Ry's house-hunting expedition. Women were notorious for sending mixed signals, but if anyone had ever accused Nick of it, he'd have sent them for a psych evaluation. At least that's what he'd have done before yesterday's real-estate tour.

On the one hand, he supported the idea of her moving out a hundred percent and had given her every practical reason he could think of to buy a house. During her attempt to do just that, he'd verbally assaulted every property, even though any of them would have suited her perfectly. It didn't take a mental giant or a shrink to figure out that he didn't want her to move out even though he knew it would be best and had advised her to make an offer.

He was feeling things that were unacceptable and against his primary rule. Survival meant not letting himself need anyone. Never get in too deep emotionally. That was the devil of it. Ryleigh had a way of skewering that rule with the four-inch heels of her come-get-me pumps.

That's why this Monday was already a freaking disaster and it was only just after noon.

Nick had finished morning appointments in the office, then looked in on a patient at Mercy Medical Center and was now in the cafeteria putting food on his tray. Halloween wasn't far away and there were a few decorations. Ghosts, witches and jack-o-lanterns were tacked up on the walls. A skylight in the bell tower bathed the room and the scattered tables and chairs in it with natural sunlight.

At the stainless-steel cashier table, fake cottony stuff made a web that held a plastic spider. The woman at the register knew him and waved him through the line. Doctors didn't pay for food, but it wasn't like that perk of the job would lift his cone of crabbiness.

Seeing an empty table in the back corner, he headed for it. Isolation was the best treatment for his condition in case it was contagious. Mostly he didn't feel like being nice.

He'd just finished his turkey sandwich and started on a bowl of strawberries that made him think of Ryleigh when he saw Carlton Gallagher heading his way. Nick noted the gray slacks, tailored white shirt and red tie that Gallagher had on along with the stethoscope draped around his neck.

Was being a sharp dresser what made the female employees in the room check him out as he walked? Maybe the sprinkling of gray at the temples of his dark hair turned the guy into a chick magnet? The puppy-dog brown eyes? Or the mysterious tan he somehow maintained even though seeing patients in either the office or the hospital made being in the sun for any length of time practically impossible.

Nick's irritation edged upward and he knew it had little to do with the fact that Gallagher's idealistic approach to the practice of medicine was different from his own. His annoyance had everything to do with Ryleigh chatting up his prospective partner that day outside the newborn nursery. Although it ticked him off even more, honesty compelled him to label the irritation for what it really was.

Jealousy.

And it knotted in his stomach when he saw Ryleigh come around the corner and weave through the tables following behind the other doctor. Clearly they were planning to eat together. When they put their green plastic trays down on either side of his, there was no denying they were going to join him without asking if he even wanted them to join him.

And the Monday hits just kept on coming.

"Hi, Nick." Ryleigh smiled. "I ran into Carlton in the hall. He was here at the hospital most of the night with the family of a sick little patient so I took pity and invited him to lunch."

Gallagher reeked of good humor, even though he looked like he'd been run over by a truck. "You don't mind if we join you."

"Nope." A lie, but he was literally between a rock and a hard place. Gallagher was wearing the hero hat. It didn't matter that hanging out for hours handholding with the patient and family made no medical difference. Nick's philosophy was to figure out the best medical treatment for a patient, then get out of the way and let it work. He was in the business of practicing medicine, not emotion.

Nick wanted to ask Ry why she hadn't made coffee that morning, but didn't want to "out" her in their living arrangement if she didn't want to be outed. If *she* brought the subject up, he wouldn't mind. All the better to give the impression she was taken.

"Busy weekend." Gallagher took the plastic wrap off his ham sandwich. There were dark circles under his eyes and deep lines on either side of his nose and mouth.

"Yeah." And that reminded him. His office manager had called a little while ago, coming down on Nick with a series of problems. It was time to spread the joy. "About Margo—"

"Your office manager." Ryleigh took a sip of her vegetable soup. "I always liked her."

"Yeah. The feeling's mutual." The tiny terror had run his office for the last five years. Fresh out of college with her business degree, she'd impressed him not only with her intelligence, but also the fact that she wasn't afraid of him. "The thing is, Margo's not happy."

"Margo raises 'not happy' to an art form. I think she likes not being happy." Gallagher didn't look intimidated. "Can we talk about the fact that her name, *Margo,* conjures an image of statuesque elegance and sophistication."

"I see what you mean." Ryleigh laughed.

"And yet there's nothing statuesque or sophisticated about her. She barely comes up to my shoulder and has the personality of a pit bull. She's like a rose—pretty to look at, but if you get on her bad side, she'll jab you with a thorn when you least expect it."

Nick couldn't fault his description. "Well, heads-up. She's ready to jab you big time."

"What have I done now?"

"You're obstructing the office work flow."

"How?"

"So many reasons..." Nick was enjoying this way too much and felt a little guilty because the other guy was at a disadvantage from lack of sleep. "Here are the top three in random order. You were on call this weekend and she needs the super bills for all the work you did here at the hospital."

"The paperwork is in the car. I didn't have appointments this morning and was here with a very sick two-year-old."

"Boy or girl?" Ryleigh asked.

"Boy. He's doing a lot better." Gallagher met his gaze. "The plan was to turn the billing over to her when I get to the office after lunch." He took a bite of his sandwich. "Next Margo issue."

Nick knew he should back off, but couldn't make himself do it. "She needs your dictation notes for your patients. The transcriptionist, and I'm quoting here, 'had her panties in a twist' when she called."

"I talked to Connie and promised to drop the information off at her office," Gallagher calmly said. "I'll smooth it over when I swing by."

He was probably good at charming women and had an answer for everything, but Nick tended to believe him. He'd had his own issues with the transcriptionist. "I saved the best for last."

"Okay."

"Margo said she made it perfectly clear to you that charts are not to be taken out of the office."

"Yeah. I got the message loud and clear."

"Not according to Margo. She did five straight minutes on wasting too much time and energy on the great chart hunt before concluding that you'd broken her cardinal rule and had them with you."

"As the physician on call, I needed the history on your patients. Why didn't she check with me?"

"You'd have to ask her about it."

"I will."

"Good luck with that." Nick almost felt sorry for him. "She isn't easy."

"Neither am I. But provoking her on purpose can be pretty interesting." There was a gleam in his eyes when he looked at Ryleigh. "Looks like I've got loose ends to tie up and the rest of my afternoon is going to get more interesting."

"Margo is a teddy bear," she told him. "You'll be fine."

"Want to come with me and run interference?"

Ryleigh laughed and shook her head. "Margo might be little, but she could take me down."

"Okay. See you later." Gallagher stood, then picked up his tray and emptied the trash into a container before threading his way through the tables and out of the cafeteria.

When they were alone, Ryleigh met Nick's gaze. "Margo certainly runs a tight ship. Maybe she gets that from you, Nick."

"Me?"

"You set that office up. You choreographed the work flow the way you wanted it. One would have to conclude that prolonged exposure to your charm and easygoing style have rubbed off on her." She struggled unsuccessfully to twist off the cap on her bottle of water.

Nick turned it for her and handed back the bottle. "Was that sarcasm?"

"What was your first clue?" Her brown eyes twinkled with humor.

"Let me guess. You don't really think I'm good-natured and charming?"

"You can be," she qualified. "But both qualities were missing in action while Carlton was here."

He was kind of hoping she hadn't noticed that. And since when did she call the guy by his first name? There was no way Nick planned to explain that seeing her with another man had seriously depleted his stockpile of charm. "I was just passing on Margo's message. In fact, believe it or not, my translation took a lot of the sting out of what she said, which makes me pretty darn charming. All in all, I'm a prince of a guy."

"I think you're in a bad mood and taking it out on him."

Maybe. The hell of it was, now that they were alone he could almost feel the haze of darkness lifting as he soaked in her fresh-faced beauty, her humor and the sweet sound of her voice.

"What was *your* first clue?" he asked, echoing her question.

"You mean besides the fact that you were taking far too much pleasure in passing on Margo's message?"

"Yeah," he said, suppressing a grin. "Besides that."

He realized she knew him pretty well. That wasn't something he'd thought about when they were married, but he did now. Apparently she could see right through his crap. Part of him felt good about that. Part of him—not so much.

"You're packing quite the attitude today, Doctor."

"Thank you. I take a great deal of pride in that."

She grinned. "Is this the hell everyone pays when you don't get coffee at home first thing in the morning?"

"Maybe." This time he couldn't stop the smile that
turned up the corners of his mouth. Nick had lost the will
to fight almost immediately after the other man left. That's
what happened when he was alone with Ryleigh.

He'd forgotten how she could always manage to lift his
spirits like this. Something warm and vital shifted in him
as he realized how much he'd missed that.

Instantly amusement faded. She was right about him
not getting what he wanted to start his day. But it wasn't
caffeine that gave him a jolt. Seeing her first thing in the
morning fed something gnawing and hungry in his soul.

If he didn't find a way to stop craving it, he would waste
away inside when she was gone. He would be everything
he'd vowed never to be.

To thank Nick for his hospitality at the house, Ryleigh
had fallen into the habit of handling the evening meal.
She cut up lettuce for a salad and washed two potatoes
to microwave while a whole chicken roasted in the oven.
Just before leaving him in the cafeteria after lunch this
afternoon, he'd told her to plan on him for dinner. But
she'd learned while being married to him that his plans
almost always changed.

She tried not to let the memories hurt because their lives
were separate now; that's what divorce did. But the sting
somehow got through her shield. That would go away once
she was in a place of her own: another thing she'd learned
when they were no longer married. In the meantime, she
was grateful to be in his house, as opposed to the hideous
hospital-subsidized apartment.

The arrangement wouldn't last much longer. Soon she'd
do a pregnancy test and if—no, *when*—it was positive,
there wouldn't be any reason to stay.

That thought stung a little, too, but she chalked it up

to how much she still loved this house. It wasn't about the owner. As far as real estate, this place set a high bar and so far nothing she'd seen had compelled her to make an offer, not even the one Nick had urged her to make an offer on. But she wasn't giving up.

Before she turned thirty, she would have a baby and a house. Her life would be complete.

When the front door opened and closed, her heart gave that familiar, excited little skip and she made a vow that when she had a baby and house of her own, it would be enough without the heart skipping.

Nick walked into the kitchen. "Hi."

"Hey. You're home." She looked up from the cutting board and smiled.

"You sound surprised."

"Wasted food is collateral damage to your occupation." She shrugged. "Being a doctor means that the cook doesn't know whether or not you'll be home for dinner even if told to plan on you."

Frowning, he walked to the refrigerator and grabbed a beer. "Would you like me to open a bottle of wine?"

"That would be nice." Again her heart skipped.

She wondered if a bottle of wine would always remind her of the night Nick Damian had pulled out all the stops to set a romantic mood for making a baby. It had been a good night.

Really good.

And a part of her wished it had been real, not just a by-product of his promise to help her have a baby.

Nick quickly and efficiently removed the cork from a bottle of chardonnay, then retrieved a glass and poured the golden liquid into it. The wineglass was decorated with logo from a winery in Pahrump, just an hour drive over the hill from Las Vegas. More memories rolled through her of going there with him, but thinking about the past was just a gigantic waste of mental energy. And it bothered her a little that she was making new memories of her and Nick even though she and Nick weren't a couple.

He set the glass down beside the chopping board on the island where she was slicing cucumbers. "How was your day?" he asked.

"I spent it with my computer and a stack of proposals for funds from Children's Medical Charities."

"When you weren't running into Dr. Gallagher."

"And you," she reminded him. "All the paperwork is a necessary evil, but it's still paperwork and has to be done. Not unlike Carlton."

"It scares me that I understand what you just said. You think I think my prospective partner is a necessary evil." Nick's eyes narrowed. "And you're on a first-name basis with him."

"It was his idea."

"There's a surprise." His voice had an edge to it.

Was he jealous?

Ryleigh put oil and vinegar on the salad greens and tossed them. Cool, calm, collected Nick was jealous? Dedicated, daring, dark and dangerous Doctor Damian wasn't happy that his possible partner was on a first-name basis with his ex-wife?

Oh, it was a heady thought. It was delicious to think that the man who had once barely remembered she was alive might actually regret that behavior. And more heady and delicious, that there was a possibility he wanted her the way he once had before reality intruded.

Surely she was getting the signs all wrong. Jealousy was powered by emotion and Nick didn't do feelings. But she was too intrigued to let the subject drop.

She put the salad by the two place settings at the island bar. "Why do you dislike Carlton?"

Nick looked up from the beer bottle he'd been studying so intently. "I like him fine. Why would you think I don't?"

"Just a feeling."

"What do you think of him?" Interest and irritation sparked in his eyes.

"He seems like a devoted doctor. Nice. Charming. Good looking." She watched him closely for a reaction and saw his mouth tighten.

"That's all superficial."

"True. And I don't know him very well. Yet," she added.

"Meaning you'd like to? Know him, I mean."

"Why not?"

"Because he's not a good risk."

She rested her hands on the granite island. "In what way? He seems like a terrific guy."

"A guy who's a doctor. That didn't work out so well for you."

Hmm. This tone and attitude reminded her a lot of house-hunting Nick from yesterday. This was the same one who'd found something wrong with every single property she'd looked at. What was up with him? He didn't want her but didn't want anyone else to have her, either? That didn't really seem like the Nick she knew, and it felt a lot like he was cutting off his nose to spite his face.

"You know, Nick, I'm really not looking for another relationship."

"Did I say you were?"

"Not in so many words. But you're just a tiny bit hostile to Carlton and I think you should be nicer."

"Why?"

He was standing by the stove, and she brushed by him to get the chicken out. The oven wasn't all that was giving off heat.

"If he joins your practice, you'll have more free time." After removing the roasting pan, she set it on the stove burner, then pulled off the oven mitts and tossed them on the counter. "Think about it. He was on call this week and you had an actual life." She stopped before adding that they'd been able to have actual sex because of Carlton. Nick might not want to thank the guy, but she did.

The thing was, Nick had brought the other doctor into the practice on a trial basis even before she'd returned to Las Vegas. Maybe he'd made the decision to scale back and have more time to himself. It was just possible that he was different from the workaholic she'd married.

"The only reason I was thinking about adding Gallagher to the practice is that there's an acute need for doctors in this valley. It has nothing to do with making my life easier. It's simply about helping kids. Some don't get time and attention if I'm the only one around who does what I do."

"You said *was*. You've decided against bringing him in as a partner?"

"Not yet. But he still has to convince me he'll be a good fit."

"Why wouldn't he be?"

Nick took a pull on his beer, then set it on the island. "Take last night for example."

"What about it? He was at Mercy Medical Center with a patient."

"Actually, he'd already evaluated the boy and prescribed meds and respiratory therapy treatment. He'd ordered all the lab work."

"That's not what you'd have done?" she asked. "I remember a lot of times you spent the night at the hospital because of a sick child. You don't become a legend by standing around twiddling your thumbs."

He shook his head. "If the patient needed me I was there. But Gallagher gets too emotionally involved with the family, with every case. It takes a toll and you have to pace yourself. Burnout is a big concern. Not to mention that if you get too close, that can skew your focus in a crisis. Especially with children."

"Well, I hope it works out. Even if Carlton doesn't pass your emotional scrutiny, you should keep looking for another doctor to share the practice." She met his gaze. "For your sake. Whether or not your motivation was about you or readily available care for children with life-threatening diseases, or both, a partner in the practice could mean you'd have an actual life."

Maybe with her?

The thought was there before she could stop it. And how stupid was that? Fool me once, shame on you. Fool me twice, shame on me.

She wasn't foolish enough to go down the same road again.

Chapter Eight

Not quite awake, Nick ran his palm over the sheet beside him and was disappointed. It wasn't filled with a soft, sexy woman. Ryleigh wasn't there. He opened one eye just to make sure. More than once since they'd split he'd imagined her in his bed. He'd almost conquered that, but the inclination had returned with a vengeance. Because she was back under his roof. But not back with him.

And it was as if two years of actively working to forget her had never happened, as if he was back to square one. If there was someone other than himself to blame, he would be very happy to blame them, but that wasn't the case. There was no choice except to grit his teeth and get through it.

On the bright side, today was Saturday and he didn't have patients. Ryleigh didn't have to go to work. Not only that, Gallagher had asked to take call. He was keeping a close eye on a really sick kid and would be around anyway.

He'd said there was no point in both of them being tied up for the weekend. Nick had to admit, if only to himself, that having Ryleigh around with two days off in front of him had more appeal than was wise. He couldn't seem to stop finding her appealing.

He felt more than heard when she tiptoed past his partially open door. Maybe because he'd been listening for her. It was something he'd started doing since she moved in. Although he tried not to, he couldn't seem to stop.

Glancing at the nightstand clock, he noted that it was half past seven. On a work morning they had coffee and a quick breakfast before hurrying out the door. Past weekends had been taken up with him being on call, the asthma clinic and house hunting. He had nothing going on and if she didn't either, they could do nothing together. And that could lead to something. Or not.

Any time now he was going to stop that kind of thinking.

Throwing the covers back, Nick got up and headed for the shower. Ten minutes later, dressed in jeans and a T-shirt, he headed downstairs. Ryleigh was sitting at the island with a cup of coffee and the *Review-Journal* in front of her, a pencil in her hand.

When he entered the room, she looked up and smiled. "Good morning."

"Morning." He poured himself a cup of coffee, then grabbed the laptop he'd left on the kitchen's built-in desk and sat beside her.

After turning the computer on, he waited while it booted up. With nothing else to occupy him, his senses went into overdrive. The smell of her just-showered skin filled his head with the intoxicating, provocative scent of oranges and spice. Her shiny hair was pulled up into a simple and sassy ponytail that somehow managed to be elegant and sophisticated. That was a testament to her beauty and grace because she certainly wasn't dressed to impress. No power suit today. Sweatpants and a "Sin City" T-shirt were casual and sexy as hell. If she needed someone to help her put sin back in the city, he was just the guy for the job.

Ryleigh glanced at his computer screen as he scrolled through the news headlines. "You always did prefer to get the news electronically."

"And you opted for print."

"That's partly because I spend so much time looking at a computer screen."

"What's the other part?" he asked.

"I have to confess." There was a gleam in her eyes. "I like the newspaper for the word jumble."

"I remember."

Nick glanced down at the page in front of her. There were four words with letters scrambled and a cartoon that was a clue. When you figured out what the words were and wrote it in, the circled letters formed the answer to the puzzle, usually a play on words. Solving this riddle was how she liked to start her day. Mental exercise.

His gaze strayed to the tantalizing territory of her neck, the column just beneath her delicate jaw. The soft creamy skin there gave him a whole lot of ideas about jump-starting the day and not one of them included using his brain. Although hands, mouth and tongue would definitely be involved.

Ryleigh had a puzzled expression on her face that had nothing to do with the word jumble. "Now that I think about it, you're still getting the newspaper delivered. You didn't start subscribing again because of me, did you?"

"I never canceled it." He shrugged. "Just never got around to doing it."

"So it was easier to pick up a newspaper out in your driveway every day than to pick up the phone and call to stop it?"

"Yeah." Agreeing was less complicated than trying to come up with some way to explain. His feelings were a jumble and she was a riddle he didn't think would ever be solved, even if he let himself try to rationalize her.

"It's your money." She shrugged. "If you want to kill a tree…"

That didn't bother him as much as killing all connection to her. The thought slipped into his mind so automatically, he figured it was a really good idea to change the subject.

"So, what are you making for breakfast?"

Her head snapped up and one dark eyebrow lifted. "You forgot to add 'wench.' Did you really just go all macho and traditional-role-assignment on me, Doctor? Automatically assuming that because I'm the woman I'd be cooking?"

"I haven't allocated roles." He was having a lot of trouble holding back a grin. "You assumed the responsibility all on your own."

"You think I did that?"

"If it wasn't you, there's been an unidentified woman in my kitchen who's been waving around oatmeal and fruit in the battle against high cholesterol."

"It's a dirty job, but someone has to do it." When she shrugged again, the word "sin" on the right breast of her T-shirt lifted just a fraction, along with his pulse.

"So, I say again, what are you making for breakfast?"

She slid off the high stool. "Just for that, you're going to help."

"Just so you know, you played right into my hands." If only.

"How do you figure?"

"If my services are being appropriated to assist in food preparation, I'm making bacon, sausage and hash browns."

"How do you know there's anything fitting that description in this house?" she challenged.

"There's a package of bacon stashed behind the yogurt and fat-free string cheese. Frozen hash browns are in the freezer with the box of healthy fudgesicles. Bad food has breached your perimeter, but you already know that since you assumed grocery-store duty." He pointed at her. "You always said calories don't count on the weekend."

"I have to admit, Doctor, you're smarter and more observant than I gave you credit for. Okay, you win. But in exchange, you've got to give me a healthy protein."

"Like what?"

"Vegetable omelets. Made with egg whites." She thought for a moment, then added, "And you're helping me cut up the veggies."

"Done." He held out his hand to shake hers and seal the bargain.

"Okay." She put her palm in his and a sizzle snapped and popped between them. Her eyes widened as she pulled back. "I'll get the hash browns in the oven and everything else we'll need out of the fridge."

Nick stood on the other side of the island and watched as she arranged the oval potato patties on a cookie sheet and put them in the oven. Then she set the stove timer. He only watched because at that moment he didn't dare get close to her. It took every ounce of self-control he possessed not to pull her into his arms. When he had the upper hand over the urge, he moved beside her. She'd assembled mushrooms, green onions, tomatoes, green and red peppers, spinach, two cutting trays and a knife for each of them on the island.

He shook his head at the assortment. "You're kidding, right?"

"Why?"

"At this rate we won't eat until next Tuesday."

"Oh, please. There's only two of us. We don't need that much." She grinned. "Man up, Doctor."

The beautiful, casual smile went straight through him and tweaked the wanting that was always there. She had no clue how much he'd like to "man up," and how much effort it took to remember that she wasn't his anymore.

While she steamed the spinach behind him, Nick picked up one of the knives and started on the mushrooms, slicing them into thin pieces. Before he knew it, the whole container was done. "This better be enough."

She glanced over her shoulder and laughed. "We need less than a quarter of that. I'll cook them all and we can have them with dinner."

"What next?"

"Why don't you start the bacon?"

He nodded and they traded places, backs to each other while she chopped and he cooked. Their bodies didn't touch, but he could almost feel her pressed against him. Perspiration beaded on his forehead and it had nothing to do with standing over a hot stove and everything to do with the hot woman behind him.

When the strips of bacon were well-done and crispy, he set them on a plate with a paper towel to blot them. He turned and saw that she had all the vegetables cut into small, neat piles on the board. She turned and looked up at him. They were inches apart and stared at each other, something hot and sensuous radiating between them.

"Do you want toast?" Her voice was husky and breathy

at the same time, as sexy as anything he'd ever heard in his life.

God help him, *he* was going to be toast because he just couldn't stop himself. He didn't even realize he'd moved until she was in his arms and his lips were on hers. With their mouths locked together, he devoured her small sigh of pleasure and it rolled through him like a fireball. Heat licked everywhere inside him.

He traced her lips with his tongue and she opened to him. Sweeping inside her mouth, he took her and felt the trembling of her body. Cupping her cheek in his palm, he slid his fingers into her hair, aching to pull it out of the tail and feel it loose around her shoulders.

The timer going off seemed as loud as a gunshot in the room and Ryleigh jumped. She blinked up at him, her eyes glazed over. He knew the feeling and didn't want it to go away.

When he started to lower his mouth to hers again, she put a hand on his chest and shook her head. "No, Nick. Really not a good idea."

"You're wrong about that. It's one of the best I've come up with in a long time."

She pulled out of his arms and backed up a step, then pushed wisps of hair off her forehead with a shaky hand. "We have rules—"

"Screw the rules."

"We talked about this. We set them up for a reason." Clouds slid into her eyes as the passion faded and doubt took its place. "As much as I'd like to keep this up, I don't want to lose you as a friend. If we go down this path, I'm afraid that's what would happen."

"It won't. I promise."

Her smile was bittersweet. "I know you mean that. You're the most honorable man I've ever met and you'd never deliberately break your word. But if we don't stick to the basics we established, you might not be able to keep that promise. And I'm not willing to take the chance."

Without another word, she left him alone in the kitchen. The insistent timer kept beeping and he turned it off. If only he could do the same to himself. He drew in a deep breath and struggled to pull himself together. It was a long time before he could admit that she was right. He didn't want to lose her friendship. His world had more sunshine with her in it.

He'd almost lost control when they were married; he'd been sorely tempted to let his feelings for her become the most important thing in his life. After she'd left, he knew how right he'd been to hold back. He wanted her; there was no denying that. She was a beautiful and desirable woman. He was a guy. It was normal.

She'd walked out on him once and would again when their agreement was fulfilled. Letting her do an end run around his defenses would be worse than stupid. Except the stupid part of him just couldn't seem to stop hoping they needed to keep trying to make a baby.

Ryleigh looked at the stick from the pregnancy test kit and the negative sign was almost an ironic wink.

Men plan, God laughs.

She could be the poster girl for that saying. Having a baby wasn't supposed to be complicated. Two friends having sex was supposed to equal a baby. Then they would go their separate ways. But God laughed.

Nick had kissed her.

A full-body contact meeting of their mouths that left her dizzy, shaken and wanting him more than ever. She'd managed to avoid him for the rest of yesterday, but that didn't mean he wasn't right there in her head. It was especially annoying when she wanted to sleep. Her idea of a good time didn't involve tossing and turning all night because he'd kissed her for no apparent reason.

Then God laughed again because she wasn't pregnant. She'd have to move back into her apartment and figure out the logistics of another try at pregnancy later. Her first thought when she'd awakened before the sun came up was to pack and sneak out under cover of darkness. But that was an incredibly spineless thing to do. Besides, except for that kiss, Nick had been completely decent about this whole thing. He deserved an explanation.

After a quick shower, she dried off, then dressed in jeans and a T-shirt with a glow-in-the-dark jack-o-lantern on the front. Tomorrow was Halloween. Trick or treat. So what else was new? For her, every day seemed to be all tricks and no treats.

She pulled her hair into a ponytail and started out of the bathroom. Her gaze landed on the negative pregnancy test stick, and a wave of emptiness rolled through her again. The feeling made her eyes blurry with tears.

"This is not acceptable," she said, giving herself a stern look in the mirror. "Pull it together."

The delicious smell of coffee drifted to her as she went downstairs, proof that Nick was up and around. There was no excuse to put off telling him about her decision.

Ryleigh walked into the kitchen and found herself all alone. "Nick?"

When there was no answer, she poured coffee into the solitary mug sitting by the pot that he must have left for her. There were no sounds to give away his position, so he must have gotten a call from his answering service and gone to the hospital to see a patient. Her being here all alone was the pattern she remembered. As stupid as it was, with him gone she felt lonely as well as empty.

But when the front door opened and closed, the surge of joy rushing through her chased away lonely and empty.

He walked into the kitchen and looked surprised to see her. "You're up."

"Wow." She leaned against the counter and sipped coffee. "You don't miss anything, do you?"

"Not if I can help it." He set a square, pink bakery box on the island.

"What's in there?" She sniffed and picked up the scent of something warm and sweet.

"Before you go all nutrition police on me, I'd like to remind you that calories don't count on the weekend. And a walk around the neighborhood will neutralize any rogue cholesterol."

"You didn't answer the question," she pointed out.

He looked at the box and there was a fair amount of guilt in his expression. "Donuts."

"Old-fashioned buttermilk?"

"Yes."

It was all she could do not to get teary-eyed that he'd remembered her all-time favorite. As comfort food went, it was the most comforting she could think of. And he didn't even know yet how much she needed it.

Without another word, Ryleigh got small plates out of the cupboard and set them down on the counter. After lifting the cardboard lid, the sweet smell was released full force into the atmosphere and made her mouth water. It looked like half a dozen pastries inside and there wasn't a single one she didn't like. She chose a regular old-fashioned, unglazed, then took a bite and savored the satisfying, but not-too-sweet flavor.

"I can get out some fruit to go with it," Nick offered.

"Not on my account."

Again he looked surprised. "Your cholesterol is probably shrieking in protest."

"We all have to live with disappointment." She ate the whole thing.

"I bought extra, but didn't think you'd actually have one."

"Really?" She looked at the five donuts left in the box. "What are you having for breakfast?"

He watched her pick up a chocolate-glazed buttermilk donut. "Crumbs, apparently."

Ryleigh wasn't sure whether or not this was the lesser of two evils, but she'd been planning to have ice cream for breakfast. "I'll save you one."

"Big of you," he said dryly.

"Sorry, I can't help it. This just really hits the spot." It was as if he'd read her mind and knew she was feeling down. "I think maybe I was craving something like this."

It was probably the word "crave" that made intensity flare in his eyes. "Are you pregnant?"

To her supreme astonishment and humiliation, her eyes filled with tears. She couldn't even say the single word. A lump filled her throat that had nothing to do with donuts and everything to do with disappointment so she simply shook her head. In a nanosecond, Nick was in front of her, pulling her into his arms.

"I'm sorry," he said.

"Thanks." His tone seemed sincere, but she wondered if that's really the way he felt. She sniffled. "It's nice of you to say even if you don't mean it."

Nick pressed her cheek to his chest and ran his hands up and down her back. "What makes you think I don't?"

"Because your first reaction when I asked for help was to say no."

"Maybe I've changed my mind."

"Have you?" With their bodies pressed together, she could practically feel his hesitation. "Do you want a baby?"

"Let's just say I'm fairly surprised. Out of eighty-eight million, give or take a million of my guys, I didn't expect all of them to be slackers."

She laughed in spite of herself. "So it's your fault?"

"Of course." With the fingers of one hand, he kneaded the tight muscles in her neck. "You and I and the internet *know* you were ovulating, so I must be to blame for failing to achieve the objective."

She slid her arms around his waist. "That's very comforting and less calories than the half-dozen donuts with an ice cream chaser I was planning for breakfast."

"I aim to please."

"Don't make a habit of it," she warned.

"Okay. Why?"

"Because such sweet and sensitive behavior could make me fall in love with you again."

"No way. You're too smart for that."

She snorted. "You never heard of that book? *Smart Women/Foolish Choices?*"

"Sure." His chest rumbled with laughter. "Right next to Brilliant men, bonehead moves."

Was he thinking about that kiss? she wondered. "Whatever. It would be against the rules and just plain awful for me to do that, so watch yourself, mister."

"Okay." He rested his chin on the top of her head. "Then I'll just have to get my mean on."

Ryleigh knew from experience that he could be cynical and distant, but she didn't believe he had any mean in him. And that was a problem, because feeling those feelings again wasn't a joke. The way his kiss had made her heart shiver and her knees quiver was proof that sparks were still there for her.

It took an unbelievable amount of effort, but she pushed out of his arms and looked up. "I'm moving back to my apartment, Nick."

"What?" He frowned. "Why?"

"I think it would be for the best."

"So, you've changed your mind about having a baby?" He ran his fingers through his hair. "It didn't take the first time so you're giving up?"

"Of course not." But she wondered why he went there. "Do you want to give up?"

"I'm not the one moving out."

She folded her arms over her chest. "No, you're the one who broke the rules."

"You're talking about when I kissed you."

"Right in one." So it had been on his mind, too. "That's not what I signed on for."

"Me, either." He blew out a long breath. "It was nothing more than a brain hiccup."

"That's the correct medical terminology?"

"It is." His tone was completely serious even though the corners of his mouth curved up.

"Define a 'brain hiccup,'" she said.

"I'm a guy. You're a woman. A beautiful sexy woman," he added. "I like you. Brain hiccup, the kiss happened."

"If you say so." Her insides were doing a little happy dance because he thought she was beautiful and sexy. "But that is exactly the sort of thing we said couldn't happen. And if I wasn't living here, it wouldn't have happened."

"I thought we also agreed that your being here was convenient and would maximize the chance of pregnancy."

"True. But—"

He put a finger on her lips to stop the words. "No buts. It won't happen again. I give you my word."

"So you're still on board with the baby?"

He nodded. "Yeah. Unless you can't handle the arrangement."

The words challenged, and Ryleigh felt as if she were standing on the edge of a cliff. There was no way to know whether or not she'd smash up on the rocks below, but she couldn't back out and show weakness. She wasn't sure she would ever get pregnant. Or even be a mother. And she knew Nick would never be hers.

They could be friends. They could be lovers. But neither of those designations would give her what she'd once wanted more than anything—his heart. Now the only thing she wanted was his baby. If she ran for cover, he might change his mind about helping her do that.

There was just one way to prove to him that she could handle whatever happened. She needed to show him that living under the same roof was no big deal to her.

"Okay, then." She met his gaze. "Since we understand each other, I'll stay."

Chapter Nine

Nick felt a hand on his face and turned his hot cheek into the coolness. He must be dreaming because he'd swear Ryleigh was sitting beside him on the bed. When soft lips touched his forehead, he decided that he never wanted to wake up. Her smell surrounded him and it was enough. Then he gave in to the tickle torturing his raw throat and coughed until his ribs hurt.

"Nick?"

That was her voice. He opened his eyes and she was there, but he didn't trust that this wasn't another dream. Too many times he'd been disappointed. "Ry?"

"Yeah."

"What's wrong?"

"You don't look so good." She rested the back of her hand on his forehead and the coolness felt really nice. "I think you've got a fever. I've looked everywhere for a thermometer. Do you have one?"

"No."

"Of course not. You're a doctor. Why in the world would you have a simple little thing to determine exactly how high your temperature is?"

"If it will make you happy, I'll go get one." His voice was a hoarse rasp and it hurt to talk. In fact, now that he knew he was awake, it hurt just to lie there and *be*.

"Easy, big guy." She gently pressed his shoulder down when he started to move. "That's not necessary."

"What time is it?"

"Eight o'clock. In the morning," she added.

"What day is it?"

"Monday."

"Crap." Just his luck. The man who never got sick managed to pull it off on his favorite day of the week.

"Margo called."

"Did you talk to her?"

"Yes."

"Did she wonder why you were here so early?" He raised up on one elbow.

"Of course."

"What did you tell her?"

"Nothing. We didn't discuss it. She would never ask. That's too unprofessional. But of course she was curious. Any woman would be."

His adrenaline surge quickly depleted and he was flat on his back again. "Why did she call?"

"She wondered why you weren't in the office yet and couldn't reach you on your cell or pager. I was sure you'd heard the phone. That's why I came in here. Margo wanted to make sure you weren't dead."

"I'm not. I just wish I was." Nick rubbed both of his hands over his face, hoping it would get rid of the fuzzy feeling in his head along with whatever hellish virus was making him feel like roadkill. "Move. I have to get up. I'm already late."

"No way you're going anywhere. You're sick."

"It's not that bad."

"I heard you coughing all night," she protested.

"Sorry." He'd kept her awake. That made him feel even worse. "Let me get up. I'll take a shower and be good as new. How about that?"

"How about no." She stared down at him and the early morning light peeking through the shutter slats highlighted the curve of her cheek, the shadows of worry in her eyes. As bad as he felt, he still wanted to pull her down beside him.

"Look, Ry, I don't have the time to argue. I overslept. Patients will be waiting."

"Maybe a little. But Carlton is there."

"He's not me," Nick snapped.

"Who is?" Ryleigh replied sweetly. "But the patients Margo can't reschedule will just have to live with the disappointment of not seeing you. Or they'll just have to wait a little longer to be seen by Carlton."

Nick had just enough energy to juice his exasperation. He was ticked off at Gallagher. Irritated with Ryleigh because she wouldn't get out of his way. Most of all he was annoyed at himself. That wasn't new, but the reason was. He was never sick, and he hated it.

"Relax, Nick. Carlton's got your back. You're under the weather—"

"Not that bad." He slung his forearm across his forehead. "I never get sick."

"I know. Iron man."

He heard the smile in her voice, and that went on the list of things that were really getting on his nerves. "Don't patronize me."

"Heaven forbid. I'm going to do something better than that."

He moved his arm and warily met her gaze. "What?"

"You'll see." She stood up. "It's a discussion we're going to have after I bring you some aspirin and you take a shower, to bring down the fever. Put the water as cool as you can stand it."

He could take it pretty cool thanks to all the practice on account of all the stupid rules in place to make sure their friendship survived the process of conceiving a baby. He was just about pissed off enough to toss her rules in the dumper and pull her down in the bed, then proceed to kiss her breathless for the hell of it and because he wanted to. The only thing that stopped him was that he didn't want to expose her to what he had any more than she already was.

She left and he threw back the covers then sat up on the side of the bed. He hadn't pulled together the energy to move any farther before she returned with pills and a glass of cold water. He took it and swallowed the medicine.

When he tried to hand back the glass, she said, "Drink it all. You need to hydrate."

She was right, damn it.

And she was right about the shower, too. He felt better when he got out. The aches had diminished and his head was clearer. Probably a function of bringing down his temp. But he was still exhausted and his throat was on fire.

He dressed in scrubs and went downstairs wearing his I-feel-so-much-better face, but Ryleigh wasn't there to see it. The disappointment arcing through him was more about not seeing her, but that made no sense. She had a job to do, too. He should be grateful she'd stayed long enough to get him up, shove aspirin at him and make sure he was moving. But he'd been looking forward to seeing what she had planned that was better than patronizing him.

Speaking of moving, he needed to get to the office and went to the kitchen desk where he always put his car keys. The usual spot was empty and he chalked it up to a mental lapse, what with flu symptoms starting yesterday. So he turned the house upside down without finding them. His phone and pager were missing in action, too. But in the search he'd found a note from Ryleigh on the kitchen island. The good stuff is always in the last place you look.

It said: *Back soon. Went to get a thermometer and other stuff. Relax. Rest!*

It was the oddest thing. He didn't even have the energy to get annoyed, although he was really going to try. Before he could manage to get a good mad on, he heard the front door open and close.

Moments later she walked into the kitchen and frowned at him. "Tell me you're wearing those scrubs as pajamas."

"Okay. If you'll tell me where my keys, phone and pager are hiding."

"I'm keeping them in a safe, secure location. Unless someone is bleeding or on fire and you're the only man on the planet who can make it better, you're staying put."

His head was starting to pound again so he sat on one of the island stools in the kitchen. "Has anyone ever told you you're bossy?"

"Yes. It's one of my best qualities."

He rested his elbow on the island and settled his cheek in his palm. "What's in the bags?"

"Soda. Popsicles. Soup. Stuff I thought would be easy going down and feel good on your throat." After putting the things away she poured clear soda in a glass with ice cubes and a straw, then slid it in front of him. "Drink this."

And then she disappeared upstairs. Moments later she was back with his pillow, a sheet and light blanket. The way she was bustling around made him tired, although he never seemed to get tired of watching her. She was small and curvy, her legs the stuff of male fantasy. She had on a long-sleeved, plain purple T-shirt, worn jeans that fit her like a second skin, and fleece-lined beige boots that hit her mid-calf. Come to think of it, unlike his pajamas, what she was wearing *wouldn't* double for office attire.

"Aren't you late for work?" he asked.

She was in the family room, smoothing a sheet on the sofa in front of the flat-screen TV. "I don't have meetings today. Everything I have scheduled can be done from here. My assistant will forward any calls that are important to my cell phone."

"That means you're staying?"

She glanced over her shoulder and grinned. "I'll be here to boss you around all day."

"Oh, dear God."

She laughed. "Admit it. Inside you're doing the dance of joy that I'll be nearby to keep your fluid levels up and feed you."

He *was* happy but would never admit it. He'd never been able to count on anyone and didn't want to start now. And the one time someone had counted on him, he'd deserted him.

"When do I get my keys back?"

She plumped his pillow, then turned and settled her hands on her hips. "When you promise on all that's holy that you will stay here and not take your germs out of this house to unleash them on an unsuspecting world."

He stood and waited for the room to stop spinning,

then walked into the family room and sat on the sofa. "I'm abandoning my patients, Ry. They're sick and counting on me. I'm letting them down."

She looked at him for several moments, a puzzled frown on her face. "Despite what you might believe, life does go on. Even if you take the time to be sick."

The pillow looked far too inviting, and he put his head on it. Just for a few minutes. "Life is different for doctors."

"You think I don't know that?" She went in the kitchen and brought his glass over, held it close enough for him to take a sip from the straw. After setting the glass on the coffee table and within his reach, she looked down. "I remember when you worked seven days a week. Rain or shine. Weekends or the middle of the night. When a patient needed something you were there. What I don't remember is you ever getting sick. Has it occurred to you that maybe this is your body's way of saying slow down? Take it easy. You can't keep up that pace forever."

She put a cool hand on his forehead and he closed his eyes to savor the blissful sensation. Beside him she moved and he felt her lips on his forehead again. Not a caress, he thought with regret, but to monitor his body temp. When he looked again she nodded approvingly.

"I think your fever is stabilizing." She smiled. "But the thermometer will make the final determination."

As far as he was concerned, her method of establishing his body temp was just fine by him. She could put her lips anywhere on him she wanted. And he really hoped that was just the flu talking. He wanted to get over what he felt for her just like he was going to shake the virus assaulting his body. But she wasn't making it easy.

She'd been sweet to his surly. Cheerful to his crabby. Beauty to his beast.

No matter what he threw at her, she hung in with him. He didn't want to want so badly for her to stay because he already knew how hard it was when she didn't. But not wanting her was getting harder to pull off. She'd definitely done something better than patronizing him. She'd taken care of him.

He couldn't remember the last time someone had done that.

Everything was back to normal a little over a week after Ryleigh nursed Nick through the flu. Whatever normal was, Ryleigh thought. For the time being it was working at the hospital and occupying space in Nick's house while waiting to have sex with him again.

But she'd occupied space in his house once before and he'd shut her out. This time she was seeing things in Nick that she'd probably been too immature and self-involved to notice before. She'd never seen him like he was with the flu, almost desperate to get to his patients—probably because this time he'd been too sick to hide it. He'd been willing to sacrifice his own welfare for them, as if something bad would happen if he wasn't there. In her opinion, that was more than a doctor's obligation. It was personal.

She also knew his stepbrother had died from cystic fibrosis and wondered if that was somehow connected. Nick had clearly loved him. When they were married, all she'd wanted was to have his love. Obviously he was capable of the emotion, but not capable of it with her.

The blinking computer cursor brought her back to the present and the work she still had to do. She was in her small, cluttered office on the hospital's second floor. There was a desk with a couple of visitors' chairs in front of it, the usual electronic equipment and pictures on the walls of healthy children laughing and playing. It was her job to raise money for programs that would keep children healthy, so they could continue to laugh and play.

Before she could dig in to the Children's Medical Charities Fundraiser Gala and the loose ends that needed to be tied up, her cell phone vibrated. It was on the desk beside her computer and she picked it up. There was a text message from the online baby center. It was simple, basic and unemotional.

Your fertile time starts in three days.

"And that means there's a five day window for conception," she said, thinking out loud.

Of all the feelings it generated, at the top of the list was, *It's about darn time*. She forwarded the message to Nick's cell and grinned like a fool. It would be fun to see the look on his face when he read it, but she'd have to wait until she saw him at the house. Glancing at the watch on her wrist, she realized that would be soon because it was past six and she really should leave. Right after she cleared up some work.

Five minutes later there was a knock on her office door and when it opened, Nick poked his head in. "You're not busy, are you?"

She swiveled her chair to face him. "What are you doing here?"

"I was seeing patients here in the hospital when I got your message. Three days, huh? Today is Friday, so that means Monday?"

"Yeah. That was from my online fertility friends."

"So I noticed."

She leaned back in her chair, a casual pose belying the shimmer and shake inside her. That wolfishly predatory expression on his face should be declared hazardous to her heart.

"I feel like the Paul Revere of the technology age. Instead of the British, it was a warning that my eggs are coming."

"Well, one hopes it's not plural." He moved farther into the room and rested a hip on the corner of her desk. "That could mean twins."

"Yikes."

"No kidding." He folded his arms over his chest and looked down at her. "So, they must have a reason for giving you some lead time on this."

"Yeah. But I'm not sure what it is. Any ideas?"

The gleam that stole into his eyes said he had a few sexy ones. "It's probably about planning."

"In what way?"

He lifted one broad shoulder. "I suppose it would be good to know if you were traveling."

"Right." She nodded; then a thought occurred to her. "Are you leaving town?"

"I wasn't planning to. Unless you came with me." One corner of his mouth quirked up. "Maybe an exotic getaway would increase the chances of success."

She blinked up at him. That would require him to take time off, so this couldn't possibly be the same man who fought tooth and nail to work when he could hardly stand. Clearly he was teasing her, but she could play the "what if" game to make him happy.

"Exotic." She tapped her lip thoughtfully. "I suppose climbing Mount Kilimanjaro would make my eggs quiver with excitement."

"What about Antarctica? Huddling together for warmth could be just the ticket."

She shivered and it wasn't just the idea of that level of

cold. It was thoughts of pressing her body to his and how easily that would work to warm her. This was getting interesting.

"Maybe a tropical island," she suggested. "Tahiti. Fiji. Bora Bora. Or Palau?"

One dark eyebrow arched suggestively. "Do you have a bikini?"

"Yes."

He nodded, pretending to consider that in a completely clinical way. "I could definitely picture a beach venue having a measure of success."

"So you think a bikini would help the boys get their game on?"

"It wouldn't be easy, mind you." He rubbed his chin thoughtfully. "But I'm sure they'd rally."

"Good to know."

"What about practice makes perfect?" he suggested.

"You're such a guy."

And that brought her straight to what she now thought of as the "kitchen kiss." He'd told her she wasn't hard on the eyes and he'd acted instinctively when he kissed her. He *was* a guy. No question that sharing a house with him was blurring the lines of their agreement, but her goal was to have a baby, not a relationship. She had to keep her eyes on the prize.

He leaned over to look at what was on her computer screen. "So, what are you working on?"

"The gala. I just got an email with the final menu after firming up the head count."

"It's never firm," he warned. "People have a way of not showing up."

"I'm aware of that. So is she."

"Who?" he asked.

"Candy Garrett."

"Again—who?"

"She's a chef, the recent winner of a TV reality competition, born and raised here in Las Vegas. The series generated a lot of press because of issues between the contestants and Candy's personal story that earned her the public's sympathy and approval. She was hired here in town by one of the Strip resorts. I got her to donate her time to do the food for my event."

"Must have been your charm."

"Oh, please." She didn't believe that for a second. "It had nothing to do with me."

"Then how did you talk her into it?"

"All I did was mention Children's Medical Charities. That's where her personal story comes in. Her little girl was born at Mercy Medical Center and she had a heart defect. The hospital had just received equipment to do pediatric echocardiograms from CMC—to the tune of several hundred thousand dollars."

He nodded. "The latest technology is far more sophisticated and has better resolution. That makes it easier to see what's wrong."

"And because of it, the doctors were able to diagnose and repair her daughter's problem before it turned into a major health threat."

"So she directly benefited from the charity and wants to give back," he said.

"Exactly. And because she was a TV personality, a lot of people are interested in the gala who wouldn't have been. It's publicity we can really use."

"Good."

"Even better?" She grinned up at him. "She's pregnant again."

"Wonder if *she* went to Bora Bora," he said.

"I wouldn't know. But you can ask her yourself at the event. I can introduce you."

"You could." He hesitated half a second, then added, "If I was going."

She knew he made generous donations but felt the event itself was all show, no substance. If something wasn't directly involved in patient diagnosis and treatment, it was a waste of his time. "I thought you'd make an exception for this fundraiser."

"You thought wrong."

She got the message loud and clear. Just because he was helping her have a baby, that didn't mean she should expect anything else. Very soon she would be able to manage gratitude for the warning, but not right this second. As much as she'd like to play "what if," she'd had a front-row seat to how easily that could lead to "if onlys."

If only she'd been enough for him.

If only he'd loved her.

Refusing to play the first time around would have saved her the pain of regret, but one thing she'd never be sorry about: She'd come out of the relationship with a boundless respect for Nick Damian. There was no doubt in her mind that his passion, dedication and commitment to doing the right thing were qualities she wanted her child to have. He was still the best man she knew and the one she wanted to father her baby.

She looked up at him and smiled, pretty sure her hurt feelings didn't show. Practice had made her perfect in putting on a facade. "So, three days. Do we have a date?"

"I'll put it on the calendar."

Chapter Ten

Nick wasn't exactly sure how Ryleigh had talked him into going shopping early Saturday morning. Well, technically he knew. Her car was in for routine maintenance and he felt guilty for raining on her parade the night before. She'd done a pretty good job of hiding her disappointment about him not going to her big event. If he didn't know her so well, the professional face might have fooled him. But he did know her and felt as if he'd kicked a kitten. In the rain. An eager, enthusiastic kitten just trying her best to do a good job.

That made him feel like crap.

He'd volunteered to be her chauffeur because she needed a ride to the mall and now he was going shopping.

Really?

The Fashion Show Mall was so far off his radar, he'd had to put the address in his car's GPS before she got in. Although now Ry was happily telling him where to go.

They were on the 15 Freeway going north, away from Henderson, when she noticed the highlighted route on the dashboard and turned up the volume.

"Get off on Spring Mountain Road," she said, about two seconds before the female voice on the GPS echoed her directions. Ryleigh stared at him. He could feel it.

"What? You don't trust me?"

"A second opinion," he said. "In the medical field it happens all the time."

"That's low, Damian. That really hurts." Her voice held a whole lot of teasing. "I can't believe you would doubt my directional capabilities to, arguably, the best mall in Las Vegas."

"What about that new one in CityCenter?" he asked, trying to deflect her.

"Crystals? It's fabulous. And expensive. But Fashion Show has great stuff at prices that aren't equivalent to buying a car or house. And you're changing the subject," she accused.

"Me?"

"Yeah." She huffed out a breath. "I can't believe you would doubt that I could get us here. That's like saying I have no estrogen."

He knew that wasn't true. She was all woman and knew how to use it. Otherwise he'd have let her rent a car while he stayed home to watch college football on his big, flat-screen TV.

"At the first light, turn left," she directed, just before the GPS chick said in point-something miles turn left on Fashion Show Drive.

When he glanced at the passenger seat, Ryleigh was grinning at him.

"I feel like I'm getting double-teamed," he grumbled. When he pulled into the tiered, covered parking structure, the mechanical female voice said, "Lost satellite reception."

"Thank God."

"Goes double for me," Ryleigh said. "If you go up to the second floor, we can park by the entrance to Nordstrom."

"Is that good?"

She made that sound women do that's part surprise and part exasperation that a man would not know something so important. "Strategically speaking and purely from a shopping perspective, this level is coveted by women across the Las Vegas Valley. Chick fights have been known to break out over parking spaces here."

"Really?"

"No. At least not that I'm aware of." She glanced over. "And it made you think about something else besides missing football."

"That was mean."

"And don't you forget it," she warned.

Not likely. Apparently she knew him pretty well, too.

He pulled into an empty space not far from the second-story walkway that connected the covered parking structure to the shopping center. Fortunately he hadn't cut off a car and no one was waiting in ambush as they exited his SUV.

As they walked side by side to the upscale department store's entrance, their hands brushed more than once. Each time he fought back the urge to link his fingers with hers. Each time the fight made him edgier.

"You know," he said, "it's not like you to wait until the last minute to get something you need."

"Last minute?" She glanced up at him with a what's-your-deal expression.

"Yeah." Must have been something in his tone. He

opened the heavy, glass store door and let her precede him inside. "You've known about this thing since right after you started your new job at Mercy Medical Center."

"It's a week from today," she pointed out. "And I've had a thing or two on my mind. Next Friday would have been last minute. Actually, next Saturday would have been worse because of the things that come up on the big day. So, I think a week out is not bad, as shopping time frames go."

"Okay. If you say so. And really, how hard can it be?" he asked, trying for optimism.

"So speaks the man who would only need to go into a tuxedo shop and rent a suit."

"I actually own a tux."

"That's right. I'd forgotten."

He let the door close behind him and looked around. If he'd stepped onto an alien planet it couldn't have looked more foreign to him. Snappy outfits all put together on faceless forms and displays of women's accessories were everywhere. Overhead lighting was as state-of-the-art as any surgery room he'd ever seen. Earth-tone marble paths led to the different departments on the floor and strains of piano music drifted in the air.

Ryleigh looked up at him. "Are you all right? You look pale."

"Fine."

"Okay. Follow me."

He didn't have a choice. The maze of racks with hangers and headless mannequins wearing sweaters and belts were disorienting. He couldn't find his way around here if the trail was marked with neon lights *and* a GPS.

Ryleigh dragged him to an area with shiny dresses made out of silky material. The sign on the wall said After Five, so he figured it was the right place. Like a woman obsessed she found a rack, then evaluated each dress in her size, one by one. The first time she pulled one out, a saleswoman appeared. It was like magic.

"Hi. My name is Lisa." The short, attractive brunette smiled. "May I start a dressing room for you?"

"That would be great," Ryleigh said.

"I'll take this and you keep on looking."

While the woman was gone, Ryleigh found five more possibilities and handed them to him one by one. Each weighed hardly anything, but together they were surprisingly heavy. She wasn't that big. He was no expert, but he didn't think any of these dresses had much material in them. The mass of beads and sequins gave him a whole new respect for the density of female formal attire.

Ryleigh examined every dress in the department. "Okay, that's a start."

"Really? Just a start?"

"It's not like buying scrubs in small, medium and large."

"I knew that."

"Right." She patted his arm. "I need to try them on now. See how they fit."

Lisa appeared and took the dresses from him. "There are chairs by the escalator if you'd like to sit. Or there's one here in case your wife wants an opinion or approval."

She wasn't his wife anymore because he'd lost her approval a long time ago, Nick thought. But he was here to make up for disappointing her.

"I'll just sit here," he told the woman.

That was a mistake, as it turned out. A few minutes of calm was annihilated when Ryleigh walked out for a full-body look. The mirror had two wings so that she could see herself from the front, right and left. That was three sides of her body too many for his peace of mind.

"What do you think?" she asked.

It was a floor-length strapless purplish-colored dress in some kind of shiny silk that whispered when she moved. Over her breasts and across her midriff there was criss-crossing material that outlined her body from chest to hip, then flared out.

"Nick?"

"Hmm?"

"Do I look like a big eggplant in this?"

He was having trouble forming a coherent thought and unstick his tongue from the roof of his mouth. Answering her question was a challenge, but he'd do his best.

He cleared his throat. "I've only seen eggplant in parmesan form, so I couldn't really say."

She gave him a look. "Don't be so literal. Do you like it on me?"

"Yes." Enough to peel it off her slowly, and that was the highest compliment he could think of. And one best kept to himself.

She turned and gave the dress a critical assessment. "I'll put it in the maybes."

Then she lifted the long skirt and disappeared. He had just enough time for a few deep breaths to bring down his blood pressure before she was back, this time in black lace. It was another strapless number with a full, ruffle-tiered skirt that stopped just above her knees, flirty and fascinating.

"What do you think?"

That he could get her out of this one even faster than the last. "It's fine."

She met his gaze and there was irony in hers. "Seriously? Fine is the best you can do?"

No. He could do better, but Lisa would probably call

security and have them booted from the store or arrested. Or both. "I like it."

"Wow. There's high praise."

"It's the best I can do. If you wanted girlfriend input, you should have brought Avery with you."

"I would have, but she's busy today."

"Doing what?"

"Actually, your friend Spencer Stone is pretty much making her life hell these days."

Good. If Nick had to be in hell, it was good to have company. "What's he doing?"

"Something about a piece of equipment he wants for the Cardiac Care Unit."

"So Avery should just okay the expenditure. She's the hospital controller."

Ryleigh pulled at the strapless top of the dress. "And she has to account for all those things. It's a big decision, but he's really pushing. So she had to work on Saturday."

"Lucky her," he said.

Ryleigh laughed as she turned away. The third time she came back, he was glad this was a public place or he'd have been a goner. The dress was white with crystals accenting the waist. Long sleeves and a high neck covered a lot of her, but that was no relief to his senses. She turned from side to side, trying to see the back. He had a full on view of her back, from neck to waist.

His mouth went dry. Sometimes it was what you couldn't see that tortured a guy the most. The thing was, he'd seen every single square inch of her skin. He knew what it felt like and he'd tasted her everywhere. Seeing her like this made him ache in places he never had before.

"I think this is the one," she said.

Of course. Because his luck wasn't that good.

"Looks nice," he managed.

"That's no better than fine." She turned to him. "Really? Do you like it?"

"Yeah."

More than she would ever know.

"I have silver heels that would be great. And a matching evening bag." Turning back to the mirror, she surveyed herself and thought out loud. "It's comfortable. Fits good."

There was an understatement. The material molded to her body like a second skin. She looked like sin in silk and he wanted to be involved in the sin, buried in her silk.

She walked over to him and looked down. "You know, I've been teasing you mercilessly since we left the house, but I really appreciate you coming with me today."

"What are friends for?" he said as casually as possible.

"I really hope you mean that, because I have another favor to ask."

He groaned and barely managed to keep it inside. She had a way of pleading her case when all his defenses were in the dumper. "What?"

"This fundraiser really has my nerves in a twist. And that's the reason I decided to shop for a new dress."

"I admit I'm not the sharpest scalpel in the O.R., but I'm not sure what one has to do with the other."

"I just feel if I look good, I won't be as nervous that night." She twisted her hands together.

"That dress should do the trick. You look—" He shrugged, at a loss for words. "Beautiful."

"Really?"

"You're fishing for compliments now."

"Yeah. Because this fundraiser is a very big deal—personally and professionally."

"Is there anything I can do?"

"You can come with me." Her eyes were pleading. "I know you hate this kind of stuff. But your physical support on the actual night of the actual event would really help me out."

"I'm not sure what I can do," he said.

"Just be there to catch me in case I fall. It doesn't seem like much, but it would really mean a lot to me."

He looked in her brown eyes, saw the way she caught her full bottom lip between her teeth. She was a vision in white, an angel who put her heart and soul into the job of raising money for children's charities. How could he turn her down?

"Okay."

Her eyes went wide. "You'll come to the gala?"

"If it's that important to you. Yeah, I'll go."

"Thank you, Nick." She bent and gave him a hug and it was almost worth the price he paid.

That was the second time he'd said yes when every survival instinct he had told him to run the other way. This not being able to say no to her was different, a little new.

And a lot troubling.

Nick was in his office, checking out the patient lab results that Margo had put on his desk. He had one more patient to see before he stopped by the hospital, then went home to Ryleigh.

Home to Ryleigh.

The whole idea of it cracked open a deep yearning inside him. And how stupid was that? How much longer would this arrangement last? The answer was simple. Until she got pregnant.

Her fertile window had opened a couple days ago, but she'd put in some late nights working on the quickly upcoming fundraiser. No sex had taken place, much to his disappointment. Over coffee that morning they'd agreed that tonight was the night. His body went hot and hard at the thought. He needed her and that thought leaked through to everything he did.

Even shopping. Especially shopping. After buying her dress, they'd walked around the mall. There was a shop with children's stuff—clothes, cribs, bedding with bears. Her eyes had gone tender and full of longing. She'd looked the same way at babies in strollers and kids toddling the aisles. It made him determined to give her one of her own. Besides his promise to do that, part of his motivation was selfish.

The dam holding back his feelings had a crack that was getting bigger every day he went home to her. He needed this arrangement to be over so his life could return to the way it had been before she came back into it.

Except he had flashes of an empty kitchen when he went down for coffee in the morning. Coming home at night without anyone there to ask about his day. He didn't like either scenario, and the sooner she left the better. Because she *would* leave. At least this time he knew up front. He'd get his head on straight this time and keep anything personal compartmentalized. He would not repeat the same mistake and come close to losing control again.

Margo poked her head into the office. "Your last patient is here, Doctor."

"Thanks." He looked up from a report that didn't list him as the referring doctor. "These CBC results are for Dr. Gallagher."

The petite brunette came farther into the room. Her hair was pulled back in a ponytail and a spray of freckles dotted her turned-up nose. She held out her hand. "I'll put it on his desk. Sorry about that."

"No problem." Just before she walked out the door, he said, "What do you think of him?"

"He's okay." Her green eyes were wary.

"Is he charming?"

Now she really looked wary. "To me personally? Or the patients?"

"Either. Both."

She shrugged. "In my opinion, he's just okay. But that could be about training him. He's resisting it, by the way. But, in all fairness—"

"Since when are you fair?"

"When am I not?" She grinned and it made her look about twelve. "You and I set up the office together. The patient protocols and paper flow make sense to us. It's not easy to learn everything without ruffling a few feathers."

"Yours?"

"Mostly."

Nick studied her. "So, he's charmed you?"

"No way." Her tone was definitely defensive. "I've been inoculated against charm. But the patients are a different story."

"Oh?"

"They love him. In fact—" She hesitated, then said, "Never mind."

"What?"

"It's nothing."

"I need to know, Margo. It could factor in to whether or not he joins the practice."

"Okay." She sighed as if about to spill state secrets. "A lot of existing and new patients are specifically making appointments with him."

"Why?"

"Some of it is word of mouth. He's been around to

community health fairs. Does informational sessions at the YMCA and Boys and Girls Club. That's general. Specifically, he interacts with the entire family, not just the patient with the medical problem."

"How?"

"I don't know." She lifted one slender shoulder in a shrug. "He knows birthdays. Remembers a kid's win and loss records in whatever sport they play. He even knows what positions they have on the team. He's just totally, personally involved with people."

Unlike Nick.

She didn't say it, but that's what he heard. And even though she didn't say it, he felt the need to justify his own policy of maintaining distance, if only to himself.

"With that level of interaction, it's hard to maintain control."

"Don't you mean objectivity?" Margo asked. "Because no one can control everything."

No, he meant control. He didn't ever want to lose it like his father had when his mother abandoned them.

"Who's my last patient?" he asked.

"David Negri," she said smiling. "Cute kid."

The one from the asthma clinic who'd wanted to play football. "Thanks for the input, Margo."

"Any time." She disappeared to go and do whatever it was she did.

Nick walked down the hall and took the file folder from the plastic holder on the wall outside the exam room. He opened the chart and glanced inside, observing that David had been in while Nick was out with the flu. He'd seen Gallagher. The other doctor had noted that the kid's team beat their archrival, also the score of that game. He also put down that David's younger brother, Jonathan, was playing football in the same youth league, a lower division.

He opened the door and went inside. David was sitting on the exam table. His mom was in one of the visitor chairs and the other was occupied by a kid who looked a lot like David, only younger.

"Hi, David." Looking at the younger one, he said, "You must be Jonathan."

"Yeah." The sandy-haired boy smiled shyly.

"Mrs. Negri," he greeted the woman.

"Marilyn, please." She smiled. "And it's not Negri anymore. I went back to my maiden name, Matthews."

Ryleigh had done that after their divorce. Nick wasn't sure what to make of that and decided to ignore and move on.

"I hope you're feeling better, Doctor." The woman's gaze was full of sympathy. "The last time we were in they said you had the flu. It's pretty awful."

"Yeah." The only upside was having Ryleigh there to take his temp and push fluids on him. It made the awful part seem not so awful. "Fully recovered now."

"I'm glad," she said.

"So, David, how are you doing?"

"Pretty good."

Nick put the chart down and removed the stethoscope from around his neck. He put the ear pieces in and pressed the other end to various areas of the patient's chest and back. There was a slight wheeze.

"How's football?"

"I'm a wide receiver."

"You're doing a lot of running then?" Nick said.

The kid nodded. "It was kind of hard at first."

"He's wheezing at night, after practices and games," his mother interjected, a thread of worry in her tone.

"Mom—" The boy looked annoyed.

"I'm not sure he should be playing," she continued.

"It's not that bad." He looked at Nick. "Coach says I've got good hands and some speed. I made a touchdown."

"Good for you."

Nick looked at him. "But you're having some problems after exercise?"

"A little."

"Are you taking your medication before practice and games?"

"Faithfully," his mother answered.

"I'm going to give you a different medication and we'll see if that helps. But we'll keep everything else the same. Drink lots of water. Stay hydrated. As long as you follow the protocols I've laid out, you should be able to play without a problem. But don't ignore symptoms," he warned. "Use the rescue inhaler if you need to."

The kid nodded. "Okay, Doc. You should come to the game this week."

Nick stepped back and looked at the boy's eager expression. Dad probably wasn't in the picture and he was eager for male approval. Nick understood the lopsided parenting. Although in his own case it had been a parental vacuum when his mom left and his dad shut down. Seeing the hope in this kid's eyes could break your heart if you weren't careful.

"I'm not sure, David. We'll see."

"I'm playing football on Saturday," his little brother said.

Marilyn laughed. "He wants to do everything his big brother does."

"Yeah. It happens."

Nick felt his chest tighten, the way it always did when he thought about his own little brother, Todd. He missed the wisecracks, someone who gave him advice whether he wanted it or not. Usually he did, especially about girls.

Boy could he use some now, straight talk about his complicated relationship with Ryleigh. It made him miss Todd even more than usual, made him wish for more time. He would never stop blaming himself for the disease taking his brother sooner than it should have.

He pulled some medication samples from the cupboard and handed them to Marilyn. "If this works, I'll give you a prescription. I'd like to see David in a month for follow-up. But don't hesitate to call if you need anything."

"Thank you, Doctor."

Nick nodded, then left the room and ran into Gallagher in the hall.

"How's David?" he asked.

"Good. You made personal notes in his chart about his football game."

"Yeah. It helps me connect with a patient. Apparently the kid's got a lot of potential."

"So do you, if you don't burn out first," Nick said.

"What does that mean?"

"That you have to separate the personal and professional or you're going to have a meltdown."

"I disagree." Gallagher draped his stethoscope around his neck. "It's important to treat the whole person and that includes family. They aren't just lungs, liver or spleen. They're flesh, blood, bone and heart, too."

"So we're still at a professional impasse?"

"Looks that way. I can't change," Gallagher said.

Neither can I, Nick thought. Margo called it objectivity; Nick believed in control. You kept your head in the medicine—everything else was unnecessary. It was just as advisable in his practice as it was in his personal life.

No one got through his armor.

"Nick?"

He looked over his shoulder and Margo was standing there, a worried expression on her face. "What's wrong?"

"Karen Wagner just called. Micah is having trouble breathing. She called 911 and wants you to meet them at Mercy Medical."

Micah Wagner was a cystic fibrosis patient in his early teens. He'd been doing so well but recently had battled a lung infection and this wasn't good.

"I'm on my way. Let the answering service know where I'll be."

He'd call Ryleigh and tell her not to expect him until later. Though she wouldn't believe it based on his past history, he wanted to get home. But sex would just have to wait a little longer.

Chapter Eleven

The night of the fundraiser Ryleigh was ready before Nick and paced around the kitchen island while waiting for him. Her stomach was in knots, at least the part not doing the cancan. It almost made her forget that her fertile window had slammed shut sometime the day before without a single attempt during the whole five days to make a baby.

First she'd been too busy; then Nick had been at the hospital with a cystic fibrosis patient for what seemed like days. Knowing his brother died of the disease helped her understand his dedication to this particular fight. Fortunately the teen was doing much better now, thanks to the world's best pediatric pulmonologist. She'd been disappointed that there was no opportunity for sex, but she had him for tonight. As a friend. And that was pretty important to her. She was going to need the support.

Pacing past the microwave, she caught a glimpse of

her reflection and backed up. She fussed with the wisps of hair around her face and fretted over the asymmetrical bun she'd fashioned behind her ear.

"I should have gone to a salon," she mumbled.

"You know what they say about people who talk to themselves."

Ryleigh started. She hadn't heard him there. Her heart pounded even harder than it had when she was just worried about her event tanking.

"No, what do they say?" she asked breathlessly.

"I'm not really sure, but it can't be good."

Nick looked gorgeous. Delicious. Scrumptious. The traditional black tuxedo fit his body to perfection, highlighting his wide shoulders and broad chest. A black tie and snow-white shirt completed his stunning look.

Ryleigh wolf-whistled. "And suddenly I'm not nervous anymore. Thanks to you."

"Congrats to me." He shrugged. "What did I do?"

"You look pretty spectacular, Doctor."

He grinned. "Thank you. But, and I'm really not fishing for compliments here, what does that have to do with your nerves?"

"You look more James Bond-y than James Bond. No one will even notice me."

His eyes narrowed with breathtaking intensity. "The men will."

"You're so wrong. At least I hope you are." She sighed at her reflection.

"I'm a guy. And I'm not wrong," he said. "What's the problem with your hair?"

"I should have had a professional do it. On top of my head. Maybe with a cascade of curls. This side bun thing isn't working. No one will want to give money to a mutant Princess Leia who's missing one of her hair bagels."

One corner of his mouth curved up as he moved closer. With his index finger, he gently traced the front of her hair, then down her throat. "Take it from me, every man in that room will be looking at you. And their eyes will be drawn to your lonely hair bagel, and your beautiful neck. That will get their wallets open and they'll beg you to take their money." When she opened her mouth to protest, he silenced her with a finger to her lips. "You're just going to have to trust me on this."

Oh my, she thought. If he kept that up, she could be in serious trouble—and not just because she'd miss her own party.

"Thank you, Nick. That makes me feel much better."

"Good. There's no reason to be nervous. You've put a lot of blood, sweat, tears and time into this. You can't miss."

Ryleigh held on to that thought when she stood at the podium in the Milan Ballroom at the M Resort. There were over a thousand invitees to this shindig, and at least eight hundred formally dressed people had attended. Along with the Mercy Medical Center chief administrative officer she'd personally greeted everyone at the door as they walked in. During the cocktail hour that followed, she'd mingled, charmed and noticed a few men who might be looking at her neck. Now everyone was seated for dinner and it was time for her speech.

She adjusted the microphone down, then looked at the audience. On the first try she found Nick and he flashed her a thumbs-up.

She cleared her throat and hoped her voice didn't shake. "Good evening, ladies and gentlemen. My name is Ryleigh Evans and I'm the regional coordinator for Children's Medical Charities.

"I could stand here and talk for hours about all the good work we do, but I have someone very special to do that for me. Just a hint—this person is responsible for tonight's menu and you're going to love it.

"You've already contributed to the children just by being here, but I'm hoping that our live auction will tempt your generosity just a little more. We have an impressive assortment of items including a year's worth of cupcakes from Piece of Cake." She waited while the room erupted in applause. When it died down, she said, "Continuing with culinary arm-twisting, we have a night to remember at the Marquis mansion—a dinner for twenty hosted by Chef Candy Garrett, of reality-TV fame. There are spa packages at some of the Las Vegas Strip's most sophisticated and elegant hotels. Weekend getaways with dinner and shows.

"Keep in mind that all the money we raise tonight will go to fund programs and equipment, directly benefiting the pediatric department at Mercy Medical Center. It's all for the kids, only the kids. This money cannot be used for anything else. And I have the best job in the world because I get to help decide where it all goes. Anyone who knows me knows that I love kids even more than I love to spend money, so please open your hearts and your wallets. On behalf of the kids, I thank you all for supporting Children's Medical Charities.

"And now I'd like to introduce someone a lot of you know from reality television. She has a story that will touch your hearts. Before turning the microphone over to her, I just have to say that if you've checked out tonight's salad menu, heirloom beets aren't an antique and no one knows what blood orange emulsion is. But I guarantee you're going to love it. Ladies and gentlemen, Candy Garrett."

While the celebrity chef told her emotional story, Ryleigh made her way back to Nick. As she was weaving through the maze of cloth-covered tables with fragrant flower centerpieces, she watched the women in the audience dab at their eyes with their napkins. Candy related her baby's early health issues and why Mercy Medical Center had just the right diagnostic equipment to help. On the big screens set up in the front of the ballroom, there was a picture of a beautiful, smiling, healthy little blond-haired, blue eyed toddler.

Ryleigh felt again the envy and the ache to be a mother.

When she reached Nick, she leaned down and whispered in his ear, "If that doesn't get these people to give until it hurts, then their hearts are two sizes too small."

He grinned and she felt an odd tightness in the center of her chest. The scent of him filled her head and his lean, freshly shaven jaw was right there. She wanted so badly to kiss him, but that was against their rules. She decided to blame it on a hormonal hiccup, just like he had.

Nick looked at her when she sat. "Is that it for you?"

"Pretty much." She put the cloth napkin in her lap. No blood orange emulsion for her. Not on this white dress. "Candy is going to mingle during dinner and personally introduce herself, sign autographs. It's good publicity for her and the venue where she works. As far as arm-twisting goes, it's not bad, either."

"When is the auction?"

"Right after dinner. I've got a professional auctioneer, volunteer of course, to handle that. He makes a living getting people to cough up money. Then the event is pretty much done except for dancing."

"So, for you, the nail-biting part is over?"

"Yes, at least until the numbers are in and we find out how well we did. Last year brought in the most money ever and set a pretty high bar. I hope to top it by two percent. Minimum."

He whistled. "An ambitious goal, what with the economy recovering."

"So you can see why I've been sort of a basket case."

"Sort of?" One dark eyebrow lifted as he leaned back and stretched his arm across the back of her chair.

"Okay. I've been crazed. But seriously, Nick…" She put her hand on his knee. "Thanks for coming tonight. The support means a lot to me and I know you hate these things."

"Can you blame me?" He looked at her. "Blood orange emulsion? Really?"

"When people come to a charity event they expect exotic, unidentifiable food," she defended.

"I think this menu will meet and exceed the expected weird factor."

This verbal sparring only happened with Nick. When they'd split up, she'd missed it. Along with the way he looked at her, like he was now. As if he wanted her. She forced herself to look away from him, afraid her eyes would give away the weakness she was feeling for him. Dinner was moving forward. Waiters in white shirts and black pants were bustling around serving salads and refilling water glasses. The celebrity chef was chatting up the people at the next table. When she saw Ryleigh, she waved and came over.

"Hi, there, Miss Mega Event Coordinator."

"Candy." Ryleigh smiled at the blue-eyed blonde in the white chef jacket that didn't do a very good job of concealing her growing baby bump. "You did a fabulous job of telling your story."

"It's easy to do when there's a happy ending. I'd like to give every sick kid one." Candy settled a hand on her belly as her gaze jumped to Nick. "Is this your husband? I didn't know you were married."

Ryleigh met his amused gaze. She was trying to figure out how to explain him and he knew it. Friendly exes? Friends with benefits? The ex-husband she'd convinced to help her have a baby? Finally she said, "This is Nick."

"You could say we're friends from Mercy Medical Center. Nick Damian." He held out his hand and she shook it.

"You're the pediatric pulmonologist." Candy's voice held traces of awe as if she were meeting a rock star or the president.

"Guilty," he said.

Candy looked from one of them to the other. "So, when she goes to spend all the money from this event, do you play the friend card?"

He laughed and looked at Ryleigh. "I take advantage of whatever I can."

"I bet you do." Candy's gaze dropped to his hand, and the thumb brushing back and forth on Ryleigh's neck. "I could have sworn you two were a couple. And I'm not usually wrong about these things."

She wasn't completely wrong, or completely right, Ryleigh thought. And it was time to change the subject. "I thought your specialty was arugula, not interpersonal relationships."

Candy shrugged. "A chef gets personal with food. People are a logical next step. And it's a shame."

"People and food?" he asked.

"No, you guys not being a couple." She absently rubbed her pregnant belly. "You'd make beautiful babies together."

Not this month, Ryleigh thought sadly. And next month?

She didn't know if she could handle more time under his roof and still keep her feelings in check.

"I have to finish making the rounds." Candy leaned down and gave Ryleigh a hug, then looked at Nick. "It was great to meet you, Doc."

"Same here."

The dinner was fabulous, even the salad, if one didn't dissect the parts and simply enjoyed it as a whole. When coffee and chocolate cake with multiple layers and fillings that was to-die-for were served, the auctioneer took the stage and worked the crowd. He did a fantastic job of getting the audience involved, enthusiastic and generous. It didn't hurt that the big screens were streaming pictures of children in various treatments at the hospital, then healthy, running and playing.

When that portion of the evening ended, they'd made almost another two hundred thousand dollars, by Ryleigh's mental tally. Even Nick had bid for and won a spa treatment at one of the big resorts on The Strip. The five-piece band had set up and were playing dance tunes. People who weren't staying for that were heading for the exits.

She and Nick were alone at the table. Her skin tingled everywhere as if she'd had a full-body massage—probably a result of Nick's touching her. If he could do that with one finger, imagine what would happen if he used both hands. The thing was, she didn't have to imagine. She actually knew. The thought had a knot of yearning growing inside her.

"So," she said, to distract herself, "I was just wondering what you're going to do with that super-expensive spa treatment you bought."

"Christmas isn't that far away. I thought it would make a nice gift for Margo."

"Mellow her out?"

"One hopes." He rested his forearms on the table as he looked at her. "And I was just wondering why you bid against me."

"Jack up the price." She smiled. "It's for a good cause."

"Speaking of causes…" He stood and held out his hand. "Dance with me."

That so wasn't a good idea. "You don't have to, Nick. It's been a rough week for you. You're probably tired."

"Not that tired." A gleam stole into his eyes. "You have to be here to the bitter end, right?"

"Until our allotted time here in the ballroom is up," she confirmed.

"Then we might as well take advantage of the music." His hand still beckoned.

"If you want to go early, I can get a cab—"

"No way. I brought you, I'll take you home." His eyes narrowed with intensity. "Right now I just want to dance with you. For old time's sake."

"Okay." She put her fingers into his palm and let him pull her to her feet.

He led her onto the parquet floor set up to the right of the tables. Sliding his arm around her waist, he pulled her into his arms, then folded her hand in his and pressed it against his chest. Even through his tuxedo coat, she could feel his heart beating and his breath seemed to come just a little faster even though the steps of the slow dance were not much of an exertion. In fact they barely moved. He just held her and she wanted to stay there forever.

It was raining when they left the ballroom. Rain was scarce in Las Vegas and Ryleigh loved the sight and sound of it. She missed that from her time on the East Coast.

But not as much as she'd missed having Nick hold her,

feeling his strong arms around her, hearing his heart beat beneath her cheek.

Dancing was an acceptable, rule-following way to do that when they'd missed by a day the chance to be in each other's arms, to make a baby. Unfortunately a missed opportunity didn't stop her from wanting him. And here in the car driving back to the house in the rain, she felt as if his arms were still around her. With his spicy masculine scent and the smell of his skin sneaking inside her, surrounding her, she felt as if he were still touching her everywhere.

Suddenly it was a challenge to draw air into her lungs.

"You okay?" Nick's voice had a husky edge to it.

"Yeah." She blew out a sigh. "Fine. Why?"

"I can just feel something's bothering you."

"Not really. Tired, I guess," she added.

"We're almost home."

She really was tired. Tired of being the rules police even though she was responsible for putting them in place. She had two choices. She could live under his roof for another month, at which time they would try to make a baby. Or she could move back to her apartment and hope he was willing and available when she was ovulating. Then another thought occurred to her.

She could find someone else to be the father.

When everything in her rebelled at that thought, she scratched it off the list. Somehow she'd find a way to have Nick's baby and work within their previously established guidelines.

Finally he pulled up to the security gates in his housing development and waited for them to open. Then he slowly made all the turns until he'd pulled to a stop in the driveway. The rain had stopped. Lucky her.

She lifted the skirt of her long dress so the wet ground

didn't destroy it as they walked inside. Flipping on light switches in the long entry, they made their way to the kitchen where he put his keys on the built-in desk.

"Do you want a nightcap?" Nick asked. "I've got some brandy. Or wine."

"No thanks." She took a bottle of water from the refrigerator and tried to twist off the cap. It wouldn't budge. "Damn it. A person could dehydrate trying to get one of these open. It's like dying of thirst in the desert with water ten feet away."

The same could be said of her soul, what with Nick so close and yet so far.

She slapped the bottle on the counter. "I didn't want it anyway."

And then Nick was there, the heat of his body reaching out to her. "I'll do it."

"Don't bother. I'm going to bed."

She started by him and he grabbed her arm, stopping her. The unyielding touch made her look up at him.

"Ryleigh—" His rough voice scraped over her skin.

"I really have to go upstairs. Now."

"Me, too. But—"

Yeah, there was always a but. The buts could get her into a lot of trouble. He pulled the end of his tie and undid the bow, then let the ends dangle. Touching his fingers to the top button on his formal shirt, he twisted, undoing it. After running his fingers through his hair, he slapped his palm on the counter. Frustration vibrated around them as he trapped her in front of him.

"I better go, Nick. Let me go to bed before I—"

"What?" A muscle jerked in his cheek as he stared at her.

"Before I can't go at all." She tried to move past him on the other side, but he shifted his body to stop her.

"I'm taking you to bed." His voice was low, husky, the tone firm. His gaze skipped over hers, searching for signs of resistance. He wouldn't find any because she couldn't manage to rally them. Not this time. Not anymore.

Her heart was racing as she stood on tiptoe and gently touched her lips to his. The soft kiss instantly exploded into flames. It was as if the whole night was foreplay, leading up to this moment. He slid his arm around her waist and possessively pressed her against him as he thoroughly ravaged her mouth.

When he pulled back, they were both breathing hard. "We can't—"

She shook her head. "Don't do this to me, Nick. Don't promise like that then back away now—"

"Just saying—not in the kitchen," he managed, struggling for air.

"Oh." She smiled and took his hand.

They held on to each other and managed to make it up the stairs. She started to draw him into his room.

"No," he said. "Yours."

She was in no mood to argue as he bypassed the master bedroom and pulled her into the guest quarters where she slept. Neither of them had sleeping on their mind.

"Here." Where no sex had gone before.

His whisper brushed her lips just before he really took possession. And she gave him full and free access, opening to him. With his tongue, he coaxed her into the heat until she was desperate to go up in flames.

Ryleigh backed up a step and frantically reached for the zipper at the back of her dress. Nick turned her and pushed her hands away, doing the task himself.

"You have no idea how much I missed doing that for you."

Before she could fully grasp the husbandly sentiment,

he pressed his mouth to her neck, shoulder and down her back as the silky material slid to the floor. She was wearing nothing but panties and silver hot-diggity-damn high heels. She stepped out of the dress and turned.

"I like your outfit." His eyes gleamed with approval and something so sizzling it made her burn all over.

"You have too many clothes on," she said.

"Easy to fix—"

Ryleigh helped him pull them off because she couldn't wait. That's when she realized that from the second she'd seen him in the tux, she'd wanted him out of it and in her bed. In what was probably a world record for speed, they finally fell to the mattress, wrapped in each other's arms.

He kissed her jaw, her breasts and down her belly. She did the same to him and had the satisfaction of hearing a hiss as he drew in a breath. His sweet revenge followed as his fingers touched her everywhere his mouth had been, then moved lower, between her thighs. The feeling was so electric, when he circled the exquisitely feminine bundle of nerve endings, she arched her back and nearly jumped off the bed.

"Easy, love," he crooned.

"Oh, Nick, I need you—"

"I know. God, I know—"

"Now. Please," she begged.

Without another word, he settled himself over her and pushed inside. He filled her perfectly and she accepted him gratefully, closing around him. Then he moved, driving into her while she took her fill. He urged her higher and higher until pleasure exploded through her like the flash and explosion of fireworks. And he was only a heartbeat behind.

He groaned, a long satisfied sound as he went still and

threw back his head. The muscles in his arms bulged and the cords in his neck stood out as release swept through him.

It was a long time later when the magnitude of everything Ryleigh had done sank in. Nick was asleep and had her wrapped in his arms. The feeling of contentment hadn't lasted long when she realized her choices had changed in the blink of an eye, as quick as the sound of a sigh.

She could either stop having sex with Nick.

Or she could stop pretending it was *only* sex.

But she had to pick one.

Chapter Twelve

Ryleigh was still rocking the glow of the Saturday-night fundraiser at work on Monday morning. The tallies were in and it had earned more than any of the previous Children's Medical Charities fundraisers. She had even more money than expected to spend on the kids.

On a personal note, she and Nick had spent the weekend in bed. Practically. She knew it wasn't about sex anymore but wasn't prepared to define exactly what *it* was. There were feelings on her part for sure. For Nick? She was only pretty sure.

Someone had emailed her a picture of her and Nick from Saturday night that was now her monitor's screensaver. It wasn't a bad shot; probably the white dress made her look good. And the way she was staring up at Nick, it was a wonder her computer didn't spontaneously combust.

He was so handsome in his tuxedo and was staring back at her with so much intensity in his expression, as if she might disappear at any moment and he was trying to hang on with everything he had. Just why she went there wasn't clear, but that was the first thing that popped into her head.

There was a knock on her partially open office door before it was pushed wide. "Ms. Evans?"

"Yes." She glanced at her desk calendar for her appointment's name. "Nora Cook?"

"Yes." The trim, attractive woman was in her late fifties and had straight dark brown hair cut in layers that touched her shoulders. Her eyes were light brown behind stylish, square glasses with black frames. She moved into the room and held out her hand. "It's nice to meet you."

"And you. Please have a seat."

The other woman took the chair on the left and settled her purse and briefcase on the floor beside her. "Thank you for taking the time to see me."

"You're the volunteer director for the Cystic Fibrosis Foundation of Las Vegas."

"Yes."

That's why Ryleigh had agreed to the meeting. Nick's stepbrother had died of the disease and when the call came in, she couldn't turn down the request for a face-to-face.

"How can I help you?" she asked.

"The simple answer? Money." Nora shrugged. "There are a lot of CF people in the valley who can't afford medical insurance for their families or lost it along with their employment. We have a one-hundred-thousand-dollar shortfall in our budget. Without those funds children won't have medications, respiratory therapy equipment or educational support and personnel to help them and their families manage the disease. And that's a very important part of keeping kids alive. Where there's life, there's hope. In the last twenty years, research has come up with drugs and therapies to prolong patients' lives and help these kids grow up. But it takes money."

Ryleigh was moved, not just by what she said, but the way she said it. And there was a profound sadness etched on the woman's face that tugged at the heart.

"Okay," she said simply.

Nora blinked. "What?"

"Children's Medical Charities will help you fill your budget gap."

"Wow. That wasn't even my most persuasive stuff. I came armed with statistics. Now I don't know what to say."

"How about thank you?" Ryleigh suggested.

"Absolutely. You have no idea how much we appreciate this."

"If you don't mind my asking," Ryleigh said, "how did you get involved with the foundation?"

Nora's mouth tightened just a fraction before she answered. "My son had cystic fibrosis."

"Had?" Ryleigh shook her head. "I'm sorry. I didn't mean to bring up painful memories."

"You don't have to bring them up because they never go away. Not really. I got involved with the organization because after my son died, the grief was crushing. I needed to do something to crush it right back, and it had to be proactive. That was a lot of years ago, not long after Todd passed away."

Ryleigh's stomach dropped. Nick's stepbrother had CF and his name was Todd. That couldn't possibly be a coincidence. "Do you by any chance know Nick Damian?"

The woman smiled sadly. "I used to be married to his father. Do you know Nick from the hospital?"

"Yes," Ryleigh agreed. "And I used to be married to him."

Nora looked a little startled. "So, you and I are members of a small club that includes women formerly married to Damian men, who then went back to their maiden names."

"I guess we are."

"The medical field and volunteer activism can be very separate worlds. I haven't seen Nick since his father and I split up." She pointed to the screensaver. "That's him in the picture, isn't it? Recently?"

"Saturday night."

"So, you two stayed friends," Nora said.

More than that, Ryleigh thought. "Yeah. We did."

"I'm sure he's a good man. He was such a good kid and really took Todd's death hard."

"He told me." Not with words, she thought, but the haunted look on his face when he'd revealed the little he had.

"I tried to tell him it wasn't his fault, but he never quite bought into that."

"Nick blamed himself?" That was something Ryleigh had never considered.

"Yes. Todd had been in the hospital with a lung infection. He finally came home and seemed to be doing okay. My husband, Alex, Nick's dad, had a company dinner and didn't want to go alone. Nick volunteered to stay with Todd so we could go out."

"What happened?" Something had or there would be no blame to be assigned.

"Apparently there was a girl Nick liked and he'd been trying to get her attention. It finally happened and she wanted him to come over and help with her math homework. He didn't want to leave, but Todd talked him into it. My son bragged about being wingman to the smartest, most popular guy on campus. He was incredibly proud of that and grateful to Nick for making sure he was included in social activities. But that night—"

"What?" Ryleigh encouraged.

"I'm sure Todd said he was fine and probably thought he was. He had been so many times before." Her eyes were bleak, even after all this time. "Nick went to study with the girl. When he got home, Todd was in respiratory distress and couldn't dial 911. Nick did and the paramedics transported him to the hospital. But his heart stopped on the way and they couldn't revive him."

Ryleigh remembered the little bit Nick had said about the incident, the dark brooding look in his eyes that told her something was very wrong. Now she knew why. He blamed himself for Todd's death. She was afraid part of Nick had died along with him. It certainly explained his heightened sense of responsibility and why he always went when a patient called, no matter what.

"I'm so sorry for your loss." She sighed. "The words seem so inadequate."

"They're not. Believe me. It helps to know people care, even after all this time."

"I'm sorry about you and Nick's father, too. So often a marriage is collateral damage because of the trauma of losing a child."

"I see that a lot through my work with the foundation," Nora agreed. "But that's not what happened with me and Nick's dad."

"No?"

Nora shook her head. "He never loved me."

"I'm sure that's not true—"

"It is," she said. "We knew each other as couples when our marriages fell apart. My husband left because of the pressure of a terminally ill child. Alex's wife walked out because she didn't want to be a wife or mother anymore. I'm sure Nick has told you how his dad fell apart."

No. He'd never said a word. But things she'd wondered about were starting to fall into place and she wanted to know more. She was afraid if she confessed that the man she'd married had kept this to himself, Nora would stop talking. She shrugged, which didn't exactly make it a lie.

Nora nodded. "Alex drank for a while and took a leave from his job. He couldn't do anything, including being a father to the son who was just as hurt and confused by the situation."

Ryleigh's heart just ached for Nick and what he must have gone through. "But Alex must have pulled himself together. You married him."

"I thought he had. It was three years later. We talked to each other because no one else understood. Then he proposed. He wanted to be part of a couple and I had Todd to think about."

"Probably not the right reasons to get married."

"Not even close." She smiled grimly. "He actually told me that he never loved me, although it didn't come as a surprise. It didn't take long for me to know it was a mistake. Alex died when Nick was in medical school. I'm convinced it was a broken heart."

"That's so sad."

"Yeah." Nora pushed her glasses up more securely on her nose. "I always wondered how Nick turned out. With his mother leaving and his father's emotional breakdown, it was such a disturbing experience and he was really just a boy, more sensitive than he let on to anyone. To have lived through that had to affect him." She sighed. "The reality is that my second husband and I divorced because he simply was incapable of loving anyone, especially me."

That seemed to be a universal characteristic of the Damian men, Ryleigh thought—although it appeared that his father at least had been capable of great love at one time. It apparently bordered on obsession, but he'd loved his first wife, a fixation that had cost him everything. And Nick had never said a word to her.

Maybe she should have sensed that there was something in his past. Maybe she should have tried harder to get him to talk about it. Instead, she'd walked away. There had to be a reason she was connecting to him again. This time she was older and wiser and knew a relationship needed a foundation. Strong foundations were built on an exchange of information.

This time she was going to try to help him find peace with his past, their past. If she could do that, maybe, just maybe, he could be the man she could count on. Clearly it was something Nick didn't want to talk about, but this time she wasn't taking no for an answer.

Nick walked in the house that evening, still concerned about David Negri. The kid was having a rough time with the asthma and playing football. If he was going to handle practice and games, they had to find a way to get the symptoms under control. But the long-term goal had to be preventing lung damage.

David had been his last appointment of the day. Again, the whole family had come into the office. The two brothers and their bantering reminded Nick of his relationship with Todd. Especially when Jonathan backed off because his brother was wheezing. The give and take instantly went from adversarial to supportive. Just like Nick and Todd. The familiar knot of regret and remorse tightened.

He walked into the kitchen where Ryleigh was sprinkling mozzarella cheese on slices of buttered Italian bread. "Hi."

"Hi." She glanced up, then did a double take. "What's wrong?"

"Nothing. Why?"

She never took her gaze from his. "That's not a 'nothing's wrong' face you've got going on there."

"I expect to get a call from a patient." Nick watched her as carefully as she was him. He waited for the hurt and disappointment to take over in her eyes and was kind of surprised when it didn't.

"I made lasagna," she said.

"Isn't that a lot of work after a long day at the office?"

"I actually threw everything together a couple of weeks ago and stuck it in the freezer for a work night." Her smile was full of sympathy and understanding. "It's warmed through, so let's eat before you get that call and have to go back out on an empty stomach."

Ryleigh filled two plates with squares of lasagna and set them on the waiting placemats. Two individual bowls of salad waited. He took one of the bar stools and picked up a fork. She filled two glasses with ice and water from the refrigerator dispenser, then put them down before sitting beside him.

He took a bite. "This is really good."

"I'm glad you like it."

They ate in silence for several moments, but it didn't seem quiet. He could almost feel thoughts racing through her head. There was a tension in her, an expectation, as if she was uneasy about something.

Finally she said, "Tell me about the patient who might call."

The truth was he wanted to talk about it and was glad

she was there. "Teenager with asthma. He wants to play football, but his mom is worried."

"Oh." She chewed a bite of flat noodles, sauce and cheese. "The boy from the asthma clinic."

He should have known she'd remember; there wasn't much she missed. "Anyway, his asthma is kicking up. He had a virus, which may have triggered the first attack, but now the weather is colder and running into the wind can cause hypersensitive airways to constrict. Or there could still be pollen in the air affecting his breathing. And I can't seem to find the right combination of drugs and therapy to break the cycle."

"You'll figure it out."

"How can you be so sure?"

"Because you're a legend at Mercy Medical Center," she said simply.

"That sets a high bar."

"You don't need a reputation. It's automatic with you."

"I can't let the disease win."

She rested her elbow on the counter and rested her cheek in her palm as she studied him. "There's more."

"How do you know that? And don't blame it on my face."

"I can just tell." She reached a hand out and brushed her fingers over his jaw. "You're quiet. Thoughtful. Distracted."

"Okay. Yes. Yes. And yes." He set his fork down and wiped his mouth on the paper napkin. "She's a single mom raising two boys. The younger brother idolizes the older one even though he calls him gopher breath."

"He sounds like a fun, funny kid." She laughed. "Is that all?"

"No. There was more back-and-forth, equally as

priceless, but that's the one most fit for a lady's delicate sensibilities."

"Oh, please." Then she said, "What about their mom? She's not offended?"

"Boys just take it for granted that nothing they say can shock her. Or offend her."

"Do you blame yourself for your mom leaving the way you do for Todd's death?"

He stared at her and realized that arrow was a two for one. One question, double wounds. Sometimes he hated that she didn't miss much. It led to stuff he didn't want to talk about.

"You asked why I'm waiting for a patient to call and the reason is because when he left my office, I wasn't sure he didn't belong in the hospital. What does that have to do with me?"

Ryleigh angled toward him and hooked her heels on the rungs of the bar stool. "Because I asked about the patient and you started talking about the family."

"So that somehow turns the situation back on me?" he said.

"Yeah. But let me add context." She tucked her hair behind her ears. "I had a meeting today with Nora Cook."

He should have expected that sooner or later his ex-wife and his father's ex-wife would meet. Both were professional women concerned about children. And when they met, it was inevitable that they would talk about the guy they had in common.

"She told you about how I blame myself for Todd's death."

"Yes. But I don't see why."

"I was older than him. Stronger. I should have known better. And I swore that I'd never let someone down like that again."

"It's not your fault, Nick. You didn't give him cystic fibrosis. He encouraged you to meet that girl. Nora said he liked being your wingman."

He'd heard all this before and it didn't help now any more than it had then. Everyone was a shrink and there was more Psych 101 coming if he didn't shut her down. "Spare me the analysis."

"What?"

"The part where you say I'm punishing myself. That I can't be happy because I hooked up with a girl and Todd died."

"No. That explains why you drop everything when a patient calls, even if it's about an ingrown toenail. You won't let yourself be happy for a completely different reason."

"Which is?" That was an automatic response, and Nick wanted it back because he knew she was going to tell him.

"Your mother left you and your father." She tilted her head to the side as regret pulled her lips tight. "Why didn't you ever tell me about it, Nick?"

"No reason to talk about something that happened so long ago."

Pity pooled in her eyes. "Everything that happens in our lives shapes who we are. How did you feel about what she did?"

Emotions churned through him, stirred up by her questions. He didn't want to talk about this, but he recognized something different in her expression from what he'd ever seen there before.

Determination.

This was a new, improved and stubborn Ryleigh who wouldn't let him get away with dodging the question.

"You want to know how I felt when my mother left?"

Frustration and rage he'd thought long buried rolled through him now. "It sucked."

"I can imagine."

"No, you can't." The closet door was open now, and no way were the skeletons going back inside. "You didn't have your folks around as long as you would've liked, but they wanted you more than anything else in the world. You can't imagine how it feels when one day your mother is the glue holding the family together and all is right with the world, and then next day she's gone. No warning. Just outta there. And everything falls apart."

"You mean your dad."

"Yeah. And you can't imagine how he felt, either." Nick dragged his fingers through his hair. "The man worked and took care of my mother and me. He was in control. Strong. Then she left and…"

Images flashed through his mind like a black-and-white parody of misery. His father drunk and not working. Not taking care of himself. Or Nick. Trying to get the man to at least care about something, even if he couldn't care enough about his own son to pull himself together.

"It's not your fault she left, Nick. It's her flaw, not yours."

It was his flaw now. "I never saw my father anything but happy, then she left and I never saw him happy again."

"Not even with Nora."

"Not even then." It wasn't a question, so she already knew his father's second marriage had problems.

Ryleigh put her hand on his arm. "You're not your father, Nick."

"I can't argue with that." He looked at her fingers and desperately wanted to link his with them. He would have, except touching her would destroy the single thread of control holding him together. "But there's no fighting the

DNA hand we're dealt. You inherited your mother's acute need for a child." So far he'd let her down there. Another sin added to the list.

"And you? What did you inherit?"

The tendency to lose his control with just one woman. Ryleigh. But he couldn't open that door; he couldn't take the chance.

Nick met her gaze. "I learned to never care about someone so much that if she's no longer with me my life will fundamentally change. To the point that I can never recover."

Ryleigh blinked at him, but the shock from his words never left her eyes. "So you won't let yourself love."

"That's a fair analysis."

She swallowed hard once, then pulled her hand away and curled her fingers into her palm. "I guess that's good information to have."

The look in her eyes said just the opposite. "Why good?"

"Because I always thought there was something about me that you couldn't care about."

"It's not personal." The lie was evident when everything in him wanted to hold her.

"Not personal would make it business." She shook her head sadly. "Now it all makes sense."

"What does?"

"Being the only doctor available to your patients serves a dual purpose." She drew in a shuddering breath. "You won't break the promise you made to Todd's memory. That means you'll be there for every health crisis no matter what. And that allows you to keep your personal relationships from getting too deep." She slid off the stool, then walked to the doorway before looking back at him. "After we met and the relationship burned so bright and hot, I thought we had cornered the market on happiness. Then things seemed to change and I couldn't understand what happened. What I'd done wrong. Now I see that you pulled back. I'd thought I was somehow the problem. That I was immature and needy and self-centered. Now I just wish that were true."

"Why?"

"Because blaming myself would be easier than knowing you just can't love at all." The sadness in her eyes said everything else.

She left and Nick was alone with her emotional arrows still making him bleed. She believed he was a coward who hid behind his patients. He could live with that.

It was better that she didn't know the truth, that he was dangerously close to losing control of his feelings for her.

Chapter Thirteen

Nick couldn't let himself fall in love.

Ryleigh would never have guessed that. Two days after that revelation she was still trying to wrap her head around it.

Ryleigh absently pushed lettuce around her plate and stared at the spreadsheet on her computer monitor. To the casual observer it might've looked like she was eating and working. She was also aggressively avoiding Nick which was actually doing three things at once. It set a high bar for multi-tasking and she should feel better about it.

Her day started out all wrong. She'd gotten used to having coffee in the morning with Nick, but this was the second day she'd skipped it—and him. By getting up before God and out the door when the sun was still thinking about coming up, she'd managed to evade him. It seemed like a good idea. She was still stunned by his personal revelations. And she felt stupid. The last two nights she'd tossed and turned, wondering how she could have been such an idiot when there were rules governing their arrangement.

She hadn't asked Nick to father her baby to get back together with him. But they *had* gotten close. Sex without ovulation meant they'd wanted each other for no other reason than that. It had meant something to her. Finding out it was nothing special to him and never would be was like getting run over by a truck. Carrying rocks.

She couldn't pretend everything between them was normal and okay. Until she could figure out what to do about it, avoidance seemed best.

There was a knock on her office door and she automatically called out, "Come in."

The knob turned, the door opened, the world tilted. Nick stood there with a file folder in his hand.

"I've been looking for you."

Well, damn. "Hi to you, too."

He was wearing jeans and a light blue cotton shirt that did amazing things to his eyes. It was just one of his extensive repertoire of sexy looks. *Double damn.*

"You left early this morning." His voice had an edge.

Was he remembering their personal conversation? Wondering how she felt? Had he missed having coffee with her, too? Maybe. But knowing what she knew now, that was nothing more than habit. The way you miss a broken-in pair of sneakers or comfortable, convenient sweatpants.

Ryleigh swiveled her chair and faced him full on. If he was really interested to know why she hadn't been there for coffee, he'd have to ask. "I have a lot of work to do."

"Is that lunch?" He angled his chin toward the salad plate nestled between the files on her desk.

"As a matter of fact…"

"I guess that explains why you weren't in the cafeteria," he said, studying her.

So, he really had been looking for her. The thought produced some heart fluttering before she successfully shut it down.

She was too tired for guessing games and just asked, "What do you want with me?"

There was a flicker of fire in his eyes, a clue he'd gone to a double meaning of the sexual kind. Then his mouth curved up. "You have money. I'm here to help you spend it."

"Of course you are." Part of her had hoped that he was here to say he hadn't meant that he couldn't care for her in a deeply personal way. She folded her hands and tucked away any lingering disappointment. "So, this is where I clarify something you already know. It's not my money. Children's Medical Charities is in charge. And someone reviews all my recommendations. Before you ask, ECMO is off the table."

"Why?"

"According to my boss, there's so much need in so many areas, a chunk of change like that should be spread around."

"It was a long shot anyway." Nick settled a hip on the corner of her desk.

"What? No argument?"

"No point in wasting energy on a lost cause."

Words to live by, she thought. But he was talking business. Ryleigh pointed to the folder in his hand. "Something tells me you have another cause in mind."

"Plan B." He handed her the file.

She opened it and saw several brochures from a medical equipment company. Beneath that there was a spreadsheet and cost analysis.

"What's this?"

"HFOJ."

She groaned. "What did I say about acronyms?"

"High-frequency oscillating jet."

"I'm guessing we're not talking the big jumbo kind that carry passengers from point A to point B?"

"No." He grinned. "It's way better."

"Want to dumb it down for me?"

"Happy to." He folded his arms over his chest. "It's a respirator that pushes a lot of small fast breaths. Oxygen flows down the outside of the tube and CO_2 goes through the middle."

She frowned. "Apparently that's not dumb enough for me. If the oxygen goes down the outside of the tube, how does it get into the lungs where it needs to go?"

"It goes down the outside of the inside of the tube," he explained. "Then the two gases mix and saturate the lungs."

"And I guess this is important."

"It is when a baby is in IRDS."

"Infant respiratory distress syndrome." She remembered that one. "What causes it?"

"Infection—either viral or bacterial. Trauma. Car accident or anything else that impacts the chest and lungs."

"How much does one of these gizmos cost?"

"About thirty thousand." He met her gaze. "For one."

She knew him, knew that look. "You want more?"

"Three would be good. Maybe four." He stood and rested his palms flat on her desk, leaning forward in his fervor. "If we run three jets, even twenty-five percent of the time, it pays to own the machine."

"As opposed to?" She was desperately trying to ignore how good he smelled.

"Renting. And there's the time factor. If we don't have

one available for a kid, there's a critical delay in trying to locate an oscillator and have the thing delivered. Then we have paperwork before getting the patient hooked up. In the long run the hospital saves money and lives."

And that right there was why she'd believed deep down that he could care for her. He fought so hard for the kids. She'd just never believed that his passion was exclusively limited to his profession.

"I'm convinced," she said.

He looked surprised. "Really?"

"Yeah. I'll forward the information to my boss along with my positive recommendation."

"That was too easy," he said. "I think I'll hit you up for a new transporter, too."

"There's no acronym?"

"Nope. Just called a transporter. It looks like an adult gurney with an isolette attached. It has a pulse oximeter, an oscillator and all kinds of cool monitors. We can bring a kid from a less sophisticated facility here for higher-level treatment without sacrificing critical care. Moments after leaving the bed, he's warm, ventilated and monitored. It's like a mobile ICU. Intensive Care Unit," he added.

"I know ICU," she said wryly. "We'll see how far the budget will stretch. I already okayed an expenditure for the Cystic Fibrosis Foundation."

His eyes darkened. "You didn't tell me that."

It hadn't been relevant information to the conversation they were having at the time. And there was no point now in reminding him of what they'd been talking about. This was business. "How expensive is this contraption?"

"About seventy, seventy-five thousand. A real bargain." He tilted his head in that coaxing way he had that was even more cute and persuasive than his argument.

"I'll think about it. Anything else you absolutely must have?"

"Of course. But I know I'll just have to wait and hope." He looked at her now-soggy salad. "Is that all you're having for lunch?"

"Yeah."

"It's not very much."

"I'm not very hungry," she said. *And since when do you care?* she thought. Being sad made her crabby.

"Are you feeling okay?"

He'd noticed her crabby and raised her a dose of considerate. That wasn't fair. "I'm fine. Just busy and a little tired. That makes me cranky."

"Try surly."

"If the shoe fits." She shrugged. "The gala was a success and now it's decision time. So much money to spend, so little time. I won't be able to cook dinner tonight."

He frowned. "That's two nights in a row."

"You miss my cooking?"

"It's not that," he said.

"Boy, was that the wrong answer."

"Not what I meant. And you set me up." He pointed a finger at her. "I don't mind eating later. Let me take you out." He shrugged. "It's the least I can do after you bought me so many new toys."

He was nearly irresistible like this, but she had to find a way to fight back. "Sorry, Nick. I can't."

"You have to eat."

"I will." She smiled. "Don't worry about me."

"I've kind of gotten used to it."

"That's sweet." She forced herself to smile. "Can I take a rain check?"

"You got it." He walked to the door. "See you later?"

"Yeah."

Ryleigh wished Nick had pushed harder to change her mind about dinner but couldn't really say it was a surprise when he didn't. One more push and she'd have been his for the asking. But he accepted a no far too easily. There was nothing in his manner to indicate anything had changed after their bare-your-soul conversation. For him it was business as usual. Business being the operative word. He was fine; she was the one with the problem.

That meant she had to fix it. And that meant distancing herself from him. She had to put herself on a Nick Damian diet. Why was it that the last bite of forbidden food always tasted the best and made you want more?

"Ryleigh!" Avery O'Neill opened her condo's front door wider. "I'm so glad you called. Please tell me you brought Cheetos, Fritos, donuts and cookies to go along with my whine. Make no mistake. That word definitely has an 'h' in it. But I've got the other kind, too. Red or white?"

"Red." Ryleigh followed her friend through the long tiled entry and into the kitchen, then set the bag of junk food on the black granite countertop.

Avery opened the glass-fronted cupboard door and removed two wineglasses. Then she gasped. "Oh, my god."

"What? Did you cut yourself?"

"No. I didn't even think to ask. Are you pregnant? Can you drink wine?"

"No," Ryleigh said, deep disappointment spreading through her. Somehow her consuming desire for a baby had gotten lost in the complicated mess of her feelings. "And give me a bottle of red. With a straw."

"That's just tacky. You'll have to make do with a crystal glass and normal portion."

"Oh, the indignities I endure being your friend." Ryleigh

smiled and it felt good. She had been so afraid Avery wouldn't be home for a spur-of-the-moment junk-food girl fest. What with her emotions all over the map, going to Nick's was out of the question and she didn't want to be alone. "Are you okay without pizza? Or something else in the general vicinity of good nutrition?"

"Get real." Avery poured red wine into the long-stem crystal glasses. "I'm going to eat my weight in chips and candy. If I consume something healthy, there won't be room for sugar, fat and empty calories."

"I see your point." Ryleigh took her wine and the bag of junk food into the family room and settled on the sofa in front of the fireplace. The gas log was lit and the warmth should have cheered her up. It didn't. "So, I'm not the only one who needs to talk."

"It's just been crazy at work and that's all Dr. Stone's fault."

"What is Spencer doing now?"

"He's relentless. Every day I walk into work, hopeful and bright, thinking today is the day he's going to cut me some slack."

"And?"

Avery settled on the sofa and opened the bag of miniature chocolate covered toffee candy bars. They were her favorite.

"Day after day I open my email first thing and there are a bazillion messages from *him*. In every subject line he has 'Urgent' or '911' or 'stat.' He thinks he's the only one with needs. Every message is a demand for cardiology. He wants more technology or some kind of phaser, tricorder thingy doohickey for the heart catheterization lab." She opened another candy bar and popped it into her mouth. "You'd think a man like that wouldn't have the time or energy to harass me."

"A man like what?"

"He sashays around like he's competing for the title of playboy of the Southwest." She chewed the candy. "Women take a number to wait in line to fall at his feet. He's like a rock star. They practically throw their panties at him."

"That could be a problem when he's in surgery. Makes it kind of hard to maintain a sterile field."

Avery looked sheepish. "Slight exaggeration for effect."

"So, he's not a womanizer?"

"No, he is. But I've never personally witnessed any panty-throwing. However, the rumor does persist."

Ryleigh grabbed a bag of chips, opened it and set it on the sofa between them. "I'm sorry he's a pain in the neck."

"You and me both." Her friend took a sip of wine and there was a knowing look in her eyes when she said, "Tell me what's wrong. And, before you wonder how I know that, it was the 'I'm not the only one who needs to talk' remark that gave you away. What's going on with you and Nick? You're not pregnant?"

"No."

"Have you had sex?"

"Yes."

"Are you worried that you can't get pregnant?" her friend persisted.

"Not yet."

Avery sighed. "At least one of us is having sex. I wish it was me."

"No, you don't."

"Uh-oh." The other woman opened another candy bar and dropped the wrapper on the growing stack beside her. "That bad, huh?"

"No, it was amazing actually." It was like when they

were first married. She wanted to hang on to the joy and excitement, but knew now there was no way to do that.

Avery chewed thoughtfully, then swallowed. "So, if sex was awesome but I shouldn't wish I was having it, that means you were unsuccessful in your attempt to 'man up' and have no feelings."

"That's what I love about you. Right in one without a lengthy explanation."

"So you've fallen in love with him again."

"Again would imply that somewhere along the line I stopped loving him. And now I know I never did."

"Oh, sweetie—" Avery reached over and squeezed her hand. "So, you're still in love with a heartless work-aholic."

"I can't really say he works like he used to. He's auditioning a medical partner."

"Okay." Her friend nodded, absorbing that information. "So now he has more time to be heartless."

"He's not," Ryleigh defended. "If anything he cares too much."

"So, what's changed?"

"Nothing. He's still the same intense Nick."

"Then I don't get it." Avery tucked her legs up beside her. "You were heartbroken because Nick didn't care enough to carve out time for you. What's different? Does he want to give it another try?"

"That's just it. I found out he never really wanted to try in the first place." Ryleigh explained about his father and mother, then the second marriage and losing Todd. "It's a lot of baggage for him to carry around."

"No kidding. The man buries himself in work to avoid coping with complicated, messy emotions he doesn't want to feel in the first place."

"Exactly." Ryleigh took a sip of wine.

"So, he's got abandonment issues."

"It sounds like a cliché." But when one was head over heels in love and on the receiving end of reluctance to commit, it didn't feel clichéd. It just hurt. "But that's pretty much right on target."

"And then he takes a chance, gets married and you walk out on him just like everyone else."

If Ryleigh had just sipped wine, she'd be spitting it out now. "What?"

"You abandoned him." In spite of the words there was sympathy in her friend's blue eyes. "I know you were hoping he'd come after you, but to him you were one more person who left."

"I thought you were on my side."

"Oh, sweetie, I am. That's why I have to be the voice of objectivity. Look at it from his perspective."

When the flash of anger flamed out, Ryleigh did just that. "Oh, God, Avery. You're right. And it's no excuse that I was young and stupid."

"Sure it is."

"No. He didn't talk about his past and I didn't push him for information. I should have."

"Shoulda, woulda, coulda. What are you? The relationship police?" Avery sat cross-legged, facing her. "It takes two people to make a couple. You couldn't do it on your own. He has to take some of the responsibility for what went wrong."

"I left because he hurt me a lot," she said.

"Not a newsflash. I was the one who held you when you cried. The question is what you're going to do now that you know all his demons."

"I'm not sure."

"Okay. Then how about this. Are you still looking for the fairy tale?"

Ryleigh laughed. That seemed so silly and immature now. But she had been that girl with the stars in her eyes. The one who believed in happy ever after with a family of her own. Now that she knew it would only happen with Nick and he wasn't likely to take a chance on her again, she figured the fairy tale had just fractured into a thousand pieces.

"No. Fairy tales don't exist. But…"

"What?"

"Before you asked what was different this time and I think the answer to that question is me."

"How so?"

"There are no rose-colored glasses. No pedestals and hero worship. No delirious giddiness. I know Nick the man. This time the feelings are just honest and soul-deep and *there*." She smiled sadly at her friend. "Thanks for not saying I told you so."

"About what?"

"That I couldn't come out of this baby bargain with Nick unscathed."

"Oh. Wish I'd thought of it. I would have said it if I'd remembered." Avery shrugged and her feisty factor slipped considerably. "You also vowed that there was no way you'd get hurt."

"Sorry. I think I broke that promise—"

A tidal wave of emotions slammed her and choked off the words. Before she could stop them tears started rolling down her cheeks.

"Oh, sweetie—"

And once again her friend Avery was holding her while she cried. In a few moments she managed to get the storm under control. After a sniffle and brushing the moisture off her cheeks, she tried to smile. "Okay. I feel better now. Thanks for listening."

"Any time. You'd do the same for me." Avery grinned, then turned serious. "But I have to ask because what are friends for except to ask the tough questions—"

"It's okay. Ask."

"Knowing what you know now, are you going to keep trying for a baby with Nick?"

That wasn't a tough question. It was an impossible one. Her yearning for Nick's baby was even stronger than when she'd come back to town.

She answered honestly. "I wish I knew."

Chapter Fourteen

It wasn't the ham sandwich and beer for dinner that Nick minded. That did its job and killed the hunger pains. What he minded was the non-specific pain he felt without Ryleigh. This was almost two weeks of nights without her there. Nights where she arrived so late she went straight to bed. Every day he expected her to announce she was moving back to her apartment, but she didn't. She just kept not showing up.

He'd been on the family-room sofa, channel surfing for the last two hours and couldn't find anything to make him forget her. It's not like he didn't know how it felt to be alone. He'd been that way all his life, with brief intervals of relief. The problem was that having Ryleigh here in the house again had been another brief interval. Nights by himself reminded him how bad it was going to be when she was gone again.

Now that he thought about it, maybe she was doing him

a favor. The less he saw of her the better. When the deal was done and she was gone, he knew exactly how long it would be before he could no longer smell the scent of her skin everywhere and want her more than his next breath. The sooner the process started, the better off he'd be.

Then he heard a key in the front door and his heart squeezed tight, like a fist in his chest. So much for being better off.

Her heels clicked on the entryway tiles before she appeared in the family room. She looked surprised to see him there.

She walked over to the couch and set her purse down. "You're still up."

"It's not late." That was a lie, but maybe it had nothing to do with the hour. He wanted to pull her onto his lap and put his arms around her. Hold her. "Did you eat dinner?"

"Yeah." She laughed, but without humor. "As it turned out, I had a sandwich in the cafeteria with Avery."

"She worked late?"

"Yes. Spencer Stone has no quit in him."

It was on the tip of his tongue to ask what had kept her from coming home to eat. Just in time he remembered the rules. This wasn't her home. She was here to get pregnant. They were friends and she didn't owe him an explanation. But he was way too relieved that she hadn't been with another man and he hated the relief thundering through him.

"You look tired."

He hadn't meant to say that. The words just wouldn't stay inside. That's when he realized how damn tired he was of censoring his thoughts and what came out of his mouth. So damn tired of the effort it took to hold everything back. But the alternative was to put himself on the line and he couldn't do that.

"I am tired," she admitted.

In spite of that, she'd stayed at work. It was turning into a habit—ever since that day in her office when he'd asked her to dinner. He'd thought about pushing her a little harder, turning on the charm to change her mind. But he'd decided against it. There'd been a coolness in her since the night he'd told her the whole truth about his past.

Maybe that's why he'd kept it to himself when he'd first met her, sensing it would put distance between them. The fact that he'd been right didn't make him happy. Withholding information probably made him the world's biggest jerk, but he could live with that. What he couldn't live with was letting her in and losing her again.

"I probably should go to bed," she said.

"Yeah. Get some rest."

"Good night, Nick."

"Sleep tight." It would be more than he could manage, but that was his problem, not hers.

She started to turn away, then stopped, a troubled expression on her face, a bruised, uncertain look in her dark eyes. Whatever had sent her running apparently was still bugging her. He wanted to make it better, but he was tired, too. And right now he didn't think he had the strength to stay on the non-personal side of the line he'd drawn in the sand.

"Can I talk to you about something?" she asked.

"How about in the morning?"

"It really won't take that long," she promised.

He'd never been able to refuse her much of anything except what she'd wanted most. "Okay."

She sat on the edge of the couch. No part of their bodies touched, but the scent of her burrowed inside him and touched him in places he tried so hard to keep her out of.

"I have a confession," she started.

"That's never good."

"As confessions go, this isn't the bad one."

Meaning there was another revelation he would like even less. "Oh?"

"I lied to you. The day you came into my office with your equipment requests. Work wasn't the reason I turned down your dinner invitation."

"Okay." He didn't want to ask her why she'd felt she couldn't be honest. The fact that she couldn't meant that he wasn't going to like any part of this.

"It's just that I really needed to talk to Avery."

"You could have told me she was having a problem that required girl talk." It was time to call it a night. "So, conscience clear. They say that's the prescription for a good night's sleep." He wouldn't know. Where Ryleigh was concerned it seemed his sense of right and wrong was never clear.

"I have another confession." She twisted her fingers together in her lap.

It was like waiting for the other boulder to fall.

Ryleigh met his gaze. "I love you, Nick."

"Sure. Like a friend."

"No. I'm in love with you." She shook her head. "I don't expect you to say anything. No reciprocal declarations if that's what you're afraid of."

"I'm not afraid."

"Then why are you starting to sweat?" She smiled a little, but it only made her look sad. "I didn't tell you that for my sake. I did it because I'm concerned about you."

"Why? I'm fine."

"You're not, Nick. I know what you're doing and it worries me."

"What am I doing?"

"You won't let yourself get close to anyone."

"Not a newsflash. We already talked about this. There's no point in going over it again." Wow, did he want those words back. Telling her *no* was like a challenge. As if she needed any encouragement to give him a piece of her mind. The old Ryleigh would have needed it, but not this woman. She'd been telling it like it was since she came back into his life.

"I think there is a point. You're determined to keep yourself safe from messy emotions."

"You don't know what you're talking about."

"I didn't before, but I do now. You're afraid of being like your father. He loved so deeply that when it went south, his world imploded and yours along with it. To keep that from happening you won't let yourself love at all."

He dragged his fingers through his hair. "Again, old news."

"I know. Believe me, you can't be more upset about this than me."

"The hell I can't." He'd tried, but hadn't been able to forget the look on her face just now when she'd said she loved him. It had taken every ounce of self-control he had not to take her in his arms and never let her go. "You broke the rules."

"I didn't do it on purpose. It just happened. And I don't want to talk about me. It's you I'm concerned about."

He saw the pity in her eyes and that pissed him off. "Don't be."

"I can't help that, either. When you love someone it kind of goes with the territory." She sighed. "The thing is, I don't think I ever stopped loving you. I ran away from the feeling before and now I realize that I couldn't outrun it." Her look was calm when she added, "I just needed to tell you. If you want to back out of our deal, it's okay. I broke the rule and you shouldn't feel like you're breaking your word. It's not fair to hold you to the bargain when you can't care the way I do."

Her serenity and certainty bugged the hell out of him. She'd been challenging him since that day in her office when she'd told him she wanted a baby. She'd pushed and nudged and rattled his cage until he couldn't think of anything but her. He cared, damn it. She was the only woman who'd ever tempted him to lose control. He didn't know how to put it into words the way she did, but he could show her.

He stood and started to reach for her when the cell phone hooked onto his belt vibrated. A call this late at night was never good news.

Nick pulled it out of the case and answered. "Damian."

"Dr. Damian, this is Mary from the answering service."

Not now. He didn't need this now. Maybe it was nothing. "What's up?"

"Marilyn Matthews called."

A bad feeling knotted inside him. "Is David having an asthma attack?"

"She said there was an accident. It's Jonathan. He's probably going to need surgery. She said to tell you David is pretty upset, but so far he's okay. She just wanted you to know what's going on. The family is in the surgical waiting room at Mercy Medical Center."

Nick knew exactly how bad it felt to be the older brother who couldn't do anything to help. "Stress can be an asthma trigger," he said absently. "I'm on my way."

"Should I let her know?"

"No. Don't tie up her phone. I'll be there in ten minutes." Nick clicked off and looked at Ryleigh.

"What's wrong?"

"David's brother was in an accident and needs surgery. I have to go."

"Of course you do." There was no accusation in her voice. That was different from before, when they were married.

"It's not like that." And it wasn't. He knew what David was going through. "There might be something I can do to help him."

"It's okay," she said. "Before, when we were married, I would try to get close and you used work to put up barriers. And I let you get away with it. But that's not going to happen this time."

Ryleigh didn't get a chance to explain to Nick what she meant because he raced out of the house. After changing out of her business suit into jeans and a sweater, she wasn't far behind him getting to the hospital. She went to the surgery waiting room on Mercy Medical Center's second floor. It was a typical waiting area. There was a TV with sound muted suspended in the corner. The perimeter of the room was ringed with chairs covered in blue and green tweed. Powder-blue-painted walls made for a serene atmosphere. But the reality was, pleasant or not, this was not a place anyone really wanted to be unless there was no option.

Nick was sitting beside David Negri. She remembered the boy who'd wanted so desperately to play football. The mother was familiar, too. Her face was taut with tension and a worry different from the asthma clinic. In her eyes, the fear was about life and death. There was no way to imagine a mother's terror, and Ryleigh's heart broke for this woman.

Nick was talking quietly, trying to reassure them about Jonathan. Ryleigh hadn't met the younger boy, but there'd been affection in Nick's expression when he'd mentioned the family after an office visit. No one had noticed her until she walked farther into the room; then the three looked up expectantly. They were anxious for good news and she wished it was in her power to give it to them. If Children's Medical Charities money would guarantee a good outcome for this family, she would allocate the funds right now.

"Hi," she said.

"You're the lady from the asthma clinic," David said.

"You have a good memory. How are you holding up, Marilyn?"

"Better with Dr. Damian here."

Ryleigh could see how she'd feel that way. There was a strength about Nick that was comforting. He didn't look like a doctor in his worn jeans and white cotton shirt. There was just a solid sense of character, that he would make it all okay. When she met his gaze, he shrugged.

"Any word yet?" she asked.

He shook his head. "But I was just telling them that Jonathan is in excellent hands. Jake Andrews is the best trauma surgeon in Las Vegas."

"He's right," Ryleigh said to them. "I've heard about him and it's all good."

"It's my fault Jonny got hurt," David blurted out.

"What?" His mother put her arm around him.

With tears shining in his eyes, the boy looked at her. "You got called in to work. I was in charge," he said, clearly upset. "I should have watched him better. Then he wouldn't have sneaked out to ride his bike in the dark. The car wouldn't have hit him."

"Don't do this to yourself, sweetie. Your brother is very strong-willed and has a mind of his own. This isn't the first time he slipped out without permission. But it will be the last—" Her voice broke and she put a hand over her mouth, to hold in the panic that was pushing to get out. She hadn't meant to sound ominous, just a mom's determination to change the offending behavior.

"That strong will of his is what's going to pull him through this." Nick looked at her, the expression in his eyes fierce and firm. "As for blame? You guys can kick that one back and forth till hell won't have it. What if you hadn't worked? Maybe you'd have heard him going out. Maybe not. The 'what ifs' will make you crazy. Jonathan made a choice. A bad one. He's paying a price. I guarantee you that *when* he recovers, he won't do it again."

The Nick Damian brand of tough love. The thing was, it couldn't be tough or any other kind without the love. Ryleigh's heart caught. No matter what he said, Nick had the capacity to care deeply and used an impersonal facade to protect himself from being hurt. He had coping skills in place and she hadn't understood that when they were married.

He did respond when patients needed him. Maybe sometimes he'd been hiding from his feelings, and he might think he couldn't love, but that wasn't what she saw. Her friend had made her realize that she was one of a long line of people who had let him down. That stopped now. He was here to help others and she was here to help him.

"I'm going to get coffee," she said, choking back her own emotions. "Can I get anything for you, Marilyn? David?" When they shook their heads she looked at Nick.

"Coffee would be great," he said. "I can go—"

"No. You stay. I'll be right back."

She walked out and took the elevator to the first floor. It was late and no meals were being served in the cafeteria, but drinks and snacks were available. On a red plastic tray, she put two cups of coffee, a couple bottles of water and sodas, along with chocolate chip cookies. Then she set it down by the cashier. After paying, she carried everything back to the waiting room.

When Ryleigh walked in Marilyn and David were talking quietly in the corner. She set the tray on the coffee table in front of them.

"Thanks." The weary mom smiled.

"You're welcome." She wished it could be more.

She grabbed the two steaming cups of coffee and walked over to where Nick was standing watch by the doorway, his body tense.

Holding one of the cups out to him she said, "This is probably the last thing you need, but here you go."

"Right back at you," he said, angling his chin toward the disposable cup in her hand. "You still look tired."

"That would make sense since I haven't been to bed." She shrugged. "I'm fine. Just so you know? You look tired, too."

"Not as tired as they are." He was staring at the mother and son and it was clear that not being able to fix their problem was eating him up.

"Do you have any idea what Jonathan's prognosis is?"

"Not really. I talked to the surgeon. The kid has a broken leg, but that's not the big problem. There's internal bleeding. Andrews has to find the source and repair it."

"How long has he been in surgery?"

He looked at his watch. "About an hour."

"Is that a long time?" she asked.

He shook his head. "Not really."

"It probably feels like years to Marilyn and David."

"Yeah." He glanced at them, and there was understanding in his eyes.

"I'm sure they appreciate your support. Hospitals are scary to the average person. Having someone like you to run interference for them means a lot."

He looked at her as if she had two heads. "So, you're not mad that I ran out on you?"

"No."

It was on the tip of her tongue to ask why he would think that, but she already knew. That's how the old Ryleigh would have reacted. The immature, self-centered, in-the-adoration-stage-of-love girl she'd been would have been hurt and reluctant to share him. She was older and wiser now. She'd learned things about Nick that helped her understand him. This was where he belonged.

Intensity slid into his eyes. "Really, Ry, it's late. You should go on home. There's nothing you can do here. I've got this covered."

"And who's got you covered?"

He frowned at her. "What?"

"Who's got your back?" she asked. "Who's watching out for you?"

"I'm fine."

"Yes, you are." She smiled at him. "And you act as if you don't need anyone. But that's mostly because you've never had anyone."

"That's me. The lone wolf."

"Very macho," she agreed. "And it looks good on you. But we digress because you're trying to distract me."

"Is it working?"

"Not even a little. I'm on to you, Doctor."

"And just what is it you think you're on to?"

"Lone wolves need—" She was going to say love, but he wouldn't want to hear that. She'd broken the rules and gone over the edge, emotionally speaking. He'd made it clear he was unwilling to love her back, or simply couldn't take the chance. She wanted that so much, but things didn't always work out the way we hoped. That didn't mean she'd walk away from him again.

"What do lone wolves need?" he prompted.

"Someone to talk to."

One corner of his mouth curved up. "I'm pretty sure wolves, either lone or in a pack, are incapable of speech."

"You know what I mean."

He leaned a broad shoulder against the wall beside the doorway. "Actually, I don't have any idea what you're talking about."

"Then let me be direct. Something I haven't been very good at in the past." She took a deep breath and met his gaze. "I can't make you love me again. And you can't make me stop loving you. But I will not leave you the way your father and mother did. I'm sticking around and I don't just mean right this minute. I'll be there for you whether you like it or not. No matter what."

"Whatever you say." The words were practiced, a standard response that indicated he was employing his finely tuned coping skills.

"I don't blame you for not trusting me. And that's okay. I bailed on you once before. As you said, there's a price to be paid for our choices and this is mine. But in time you'll see that I'm not going anywhere."

He ran his fingers through his hair and he got that look in his eyes. The same one he had when talking about how his brother died. "What makes you think I won't bail on you?"

"Because I know what kind of man you are. I believe in you."

There were doubts in his mind. She could almost see him ticking them off. But before she could go there, a man walked into the room. He had dark hair, gray eyes and was wearing scrubs. He looked tired, too.

Instantly, Marilyn and David stood and walked over to him. Nick straightened away from the wall, and before anyone else could ask he said, "Jake, how'd the surgery go? How's Jonathan?"

Chapter Fifteen

Nick felt Ryleigh move close; then her fingers slipped into his hand and squeezed. When Jake smiled, relief edged through him.

The surgeon looked at Marilyn who had her arm around David's shoulders. "Your son is going to be fine. I repaired a laceration in his liver. He lost some blood and will be sore, but the organ is one of the most resilient in the body. He's young and strong—"

"And strong-willed," Nick added.

"That's good." Jake nodded. "His prognosis is excellent. Barring unforeseen complications, he should be good as new."

"Oh, thank God." Marilyn put a trembling hand to her mouth, then squeezed her son. "When he's recuperated, I'm grounding him for the rest of his life."

"I'm sure he's learned a lesson," Jake said.

"When can we see him?"

"He's in recovery and should be waking up soon. There's a waiting room right outside. I'll have one of the nurses bring you in when he's ready."

"Thank you, Doctor. The words seem so inadequate, but I've never meant them more in my life."

"You're welcome. I'll see you in a few minutes." Jake nodded, then walked out.

Nick gave Ryleigh's fingers a squeeze before letting her go so David could give him a high five. Then the boy threw himself into Nick's arms.

"Thanks." Emotion was thick in his voice.

A lump in his own throat, Nick cupped the back of his head before ruffling the kid's hair. "For what?"

"Being here." David looked up, tears in his eyes. "I just knew it would be okay when you came."

"Dr. Andrews is the man of the hour."

"Yeah, he did good. But you—"

"David's right. You kept us steady. Sometimes his asthma flares up when he's anxious, but that didn't happen." Marilyn hugged him. "You didn't have to, but I knew you'd come. That made all the difference. I could be strong for both my boys."

"I'm glad." He watched them walk to the waiting room doorway. "I'll check in on you guys in a little while."

She nodded. Then they were gone and he was alone with Ryleigh.

When Nick looked at her, she was brushing away the moisture on her cheeks. "Are you crying?"

"I love happy endings." Her voice trembled with emotion. "And you, Doctor, are such a knight in shining armor."

"But I didn't do anything," he insisted.

"You simply cared. The merits of that in terms of that

medical benefit can't be quantified." The last word came out through a yawn she couldn't hold back. "Sorry."

"That's it. Time for you to stand down." There were circles under her eyes, giving her a fragile look that made him want to wrap her in his arms and keep her safe.

"Okay," she said. "If you're sure you don't need me."

Of course he needed her. That was the hell of it. He hadn't really understood how much he needed her until she was gone. And she'd gone because he pushed her away.

Something shifted between them; he could feel it. But hope didn't come easily to him. In spite of the sincere speech about loving him and sticking around, he always prepared for the worst, in this case, the worst being that he was losing her all over again.

"Go get some rest."

"Okay." She stood on tiptoe and kissed his cheek, then left the waiting room.

Nick was alone. He should be used to it, but Ryleigh had changed that. The fragrance she'd left behind seemed to mock him. So he would do what he always did. Hide behind work. On his way to the recovery room he rounded a corner and almost literally ran into Carlton Gallagher. The other guy was in jeans and a black T-shirt, and had a stethoscope draped around his neck.

"Nick? What are you doing here? Did I get the call schedule screwed up?"

"No. The answering service passed on a message from Marilyn Matthews that Jonathan Negri was here and needed surgery."

"What? Why?"

"An accident. As scores go, it's car one, boy on bike nothing." Nick added, "He's in recovery now. Jake Andrews says he'll be fine."

Gallagher looked more and more surprised, clearly

understanding that Nick wasn't there to treat a medical emergency. "I say again, what are you doing here?"

Nick rubbed a hand over the back of his neck. "You first."

"I'm looking in on a patient who came into pediatric emergency. He's got bilateral pneumonia and I wanted to make sure they get his temp down."

"Always going the extra mile."

Gallagher looked irritated. Or tired. Or both. "Okay, Nick, I know we have a philosophical difference regarding the emotional component in practicing medicine. We tried working together and it didn't work. Maybe we should just give it up. No hard feelings."

"Not so fast."

"Why not?" The other man scowled, a change from the easygoing doctor. "I'm letting you off the hook. No harm, no foul. I'll bow out gracefully."

"I'd rather you didn't."

"Look, it's late and I'm in no mood for jokes."

"I've never been more serious." Nick smiled. "And that's saying a lot for me."

"I don't understand." Carlton leaned against the wall. He was definitely tired. There was a lot of that going around.

"You have an interesting style and I could learn a lot from you."

"Like what?"

Nick folded his arms over his chest. "For starters, there's a portion of practicing medicine that isn't about tests, treatment and prescriptions. It's about heart."

The other man smiled slowly. "I couldn't agree more."

"Sounds to me like a good start for a medical partnership. You're just the guy I need and I don't want to lose you because I've been a pigheaded ass."

"I couldn't agree more."

Nick laughed. "I'll have my lawyer draw up a contract. Welcome to the practice, Doctor."

Gallagher held out his hand, and they sealed the deal, then resumed walking toward the recovery room.

"So," Carlton said, "to what do I owe this change of heart?"

"You can't change a heart when you don't have one."

"That's bull. Something's going on with you, and if I had to guess, I'd say it's Ryleigh."

"Don't go there," Nick warned.

"Can't help it. I'm wired that way. You better get used to it. Unless you want to take back the partnership offer."

"No."

"Then what's up with you and Ryleigh?"

Besides his bargain to get her pregnant and failing? Too much information. But the guy was into feelings and had seen through his. It was easier not to deny it. "We're just going through a thing."

"A thing?" Gallagher gave him a look. "A thing as in you really like her?"

"Maybe."

"You're not so good with words, are you?"

Nick shrugged. "It's a flaw."

"I couldn't agree more." Gallagher grinned.

"I'm working on it."

"Then start by telling her how you feel."

"I messed up when we were married." Nick remembered a mother's emotional gratitude just a while ago when she'd said words were inadequate. He knew exactly what she meant. Ry had said she loved him, but that didn't mean she would ever be his. "It's not likely she'll trust me again."

"Meaning you're afraid to put yourself out there again."

"You know, Carlton, career trajectory in a medical practice could be aborted when you call the senior partner a coward."

"Yeah. I'm really scared." His tone said just the opposite. "The thing is she cares about you and you care about her."

A lot of people who supposedly cared about him had disappeared. "How do you know that, and what's your point?"

"I could tell the first time I met her and you wanted to rip my head off." He held up his hand to ward off the protest. "You were jealous as hell. The point is you need to bare your soul to the lady."

"You did not really just say that to me."

"Yeah. I did. And here's why. We're pulmonologists. We treat kids with chronic lung problems, not only in a crisis, but to help them manage diseases in a way that will preserve organ function. We do that to give them the best possible quality of life. Same with you."

"I don't get it."

"Then let me connect the dots," Carlton said patiently. "You're going through the motions of living. Unless you're honest with her, you've only got half a life." He stopped at the double doors to the recovery room. "For what it's worth that's my diagnosis and treatment. I'm going to check on Jonathan. You coming?"

"In a minute."

The other man pushed through the doors, but Nick held back. He hated like hell to admit it, but his new partner was right. To get what he wanted, he had to let go of his control and let Ryleigh in. It *was* a risk, but to not take it would mean he'd lose her for sure.

His professional life was falling into place with a new associate to share the load. It was just a bonus that Dr. Gallagher was a pretty good judge of character and had a knack for connecting dots.

He'd booted Nick in the ass and made him face what he'd known the minute he saw Ryleigh again. She was the only woman he had ever wanted. He'd been a pigheaded jerk and let her get away once, but no one, not even Gallagher, could say he didn't learn from his mistakes.

"You look terrible."

"Thank you so much," Ryleigh said. The next morning she sat across a hospital cafeteria table from her friend Avery. "It's really a confidence boost to start your day knowing you look like something the cat yakked up."

"That's not what I meant and you know it. Someone got up on the crabby side of the bed this morning. Premenstrual tension?"

"Probably." Ryleigh looked down at the dry English muffin and orange juice on her tray and her stomach did an unhappy little clench.

Avery didn't miss the reaction. "Are you feeling all right?"

"Yeah. A little tired. I was here at the hospital kind of late last night with Nick."

"Something wrong?"

"Not with us. Just the usual. He won't let himself love me, but that's not news." She sighed and willed herself not to be a whiner. "A patient of his, actually the younger brother of his patient, was hit by a car when he was on his bike."

Avery looked concerned. "How is he?"

"Doing fine. The trauma surgeon fixed him up and he's going to make a full recovery. I'm sure between now and the time he's a grown man, his mother will spend a fortune on hair product to cover the gray."

"Sounds like it. But—" Avery looked puzzled. "That's not Nick's specialty. Why was he here?"

"Nick came to emotionally support the asthmatic older brother who is his patient. And I came to support Nick."

Avery speared a piece of melon from her fruit salad, then popped it in her mouth and chewed thoughtfully. "That's different for him, isn't it?"

"What?"

"Well, from what you told me, he keeps an emotional distance from everyone, including his patients. He's like a car mechanic, only with people, little people."

"It's a fact that children are not small adults and can't be medically treated the same."

"I know." Avery chewed and swallowed a strawberry before continuing. "What I'm saying is that when a car breaks down, the mechanic fixes the problem. But it's a car so there's no emotion involved. According to you, Nick never turned his back when needed, but always holds his emotions in check. He fixes kids and is an awesome doctor who acts like a mechanic."

"I'm not sure it's an appropriate comparison, but essentially you're right." Ryleigh broke off a piece of dry muffin and rolled it between her fingers. "There was no medical reason for him to be here last night. It was all emotion. Something about the two brothers got to him."

"So something is changing with him. Any ideas what's going on?"

"Well, I told him I was in love with him."

Avery's eyes widened. "That could start a chain reaction with the potential for emotional growth. It reminds me of the lyrics from a song…you know the one about how the two people are not really friends, but then one changes when the other least expects it.…"

"Not likely in our case. I told Nick that he didn't have to follow through on the baby bargain and I'd still always be there for him. It doesn't matter that he can't love me back."

"That explains why you were here with him last night."

"Exactly." Ryleigh dropped the mangled piece of muffin on her plate.

"What time did you get back to his place?"

"Actually I stayed at my apartment because it's two minutes from the hospital and I was pretty tired. It was about eleven-thirty. Why?"

"Because you've got dark circles under your eyes and that's not really so late." Avery studied the mutilated English muffin and orange juice. "Where's your coffee? You never met a cup you didn't like."

"It just didn't sound good." Ryleigh made a face. "The smell of it when I walked in here made my stomach turn."

"Oh my."

There was some kind of aha-I've-got-it expression on her friend's face, but Ryleigh was clueless. "What?"

"You're pregnant."

Ryleigh froze and stared. Then she vehemently shook her head. "No way."

"What no way? You've been having unprotected sex with Nick Damian."

Ryleigh shushed her, then looked around at the sprinkling of hospital employees occupying nearby tables. "Say it a little louder. I don't think they heard you on the other side of the room."

Avery bent closer and in a voice barely above a whisper

said, "Have you or have you not been sleeping with Nick?"

"Yes. But when we were last together I wasn't ovulating. We just barely missed my fertile time."

"And you knew this when you slept with him?"

"Yes."

"So it was just because—"

"I wanted to. Yes," Ryleigh confirmed.

"How do you know you missed ovulation?"

"My email alert said so."

"When charting one's fertility online, one must expect a margin of error." Avery looked skeptical; then she looked annoyed. "What's *he* doing here?"

Looking over her shoulder, Ryleigh followed her friend's gaze and saw Spencer Stone, Mercy Medical Center's foremost cardiac specialist and target of panty-throwing groupies. She started to wave him over, and Avery hissed a warning.

"No. That man is the bane of my existence." She hunched down, trying to make herself smaller. "What's he doing slumming in the cafeteria instead of meeting his peers in the doctor's dining room?"

"Maybe he's looking for you."

The man had dark blond hair and piercing green eyes. He was tall and broad-shouldered, a football player's build.

"I wonder if he would be interested in having a baby."

Avery looked horrified. "Bite your tongue. You're in love with Nick. And Spencer Stoneheart still thinks he's the big man on campus females cannot say no to."

"But you say no on a regular basis. Good thing you're around to give him balance," Ryleigh said.

"I'm not going to be around." Avery watched the doctor

leave, then stood. "I'm going to hide. Before I do, I have a suggestion."

"Which is?"

"If I were you, I'd do a pregnancy test."

The next morning Ryleigh stared at the test stick. She'd left a message on Nick's voice mail that she was spending another night at her apartment because she had things to do there. It wasn't a lie. Avery had put doubts in her mind and before she saw Nick again, she wanted to know for sure.

And now she did.

She left the test stick on the bathroom counter, went to the living room and sat on the horrid couch. Her state of shock had nothing to do with the hideously decorated apartment and everything to do with the test. Before doing it, she'd carefully studied the instructions. She'd waited until morning, the optimum time for accuracy and memorized all the factors that could cause a false negative. She'd been prepared for that. She'd already seen the minus and knew how disappointment felt. Nick had been there to cheer her up.

This time she didn't need cheering up. Or maybe she did.

"Pregnant," she whispered.

She was having Nick's baby, a child conceived in love. At least for her. Him? Not so much. And that's when the tears started.

"Oh, for crying out loud," she said, swiping at her cheeks.

Then the doorbell rang. She was tempted to ignore it until there was a knock followed by Nick's voice.

"Ryleigh? I know you're in there. Your car is in the parking lot."

"Oh, for crying out loud," she said to herself. Then, louder, she called out, "Coming."

She scrubbed her fingers beneath her eyes to remove the traces of tears. Still wearing the sweatpants and long-sleeved T-shirt she'd slept in, she walked to the door. Her hair wasn't brushed and the only cosmetic on her face was night cream that was long gone. The words "worst-case scenario" came to mind. When those words came to mind, a woman wanted to look her absolute best.

"Ryleigh?"

That was not the tone of a tolerant and long-suffering man who would patiently wait for her to freshen up. She opened the door and they both spoke at the same time.

"I have something to tell you—"

"You need to listen to me—"

"I'm going first." Nick's anxious gaze dragged over her from head to toe as if he hadn't seen her in years. "I'd appreciate it if you didn't interrupt me."

"Okay." She closed the door, then folded her arms over her chest and looked up at him. It was so good to see him, and she felt a familiar tightness just beneath her heart.

He took a deep breath. "You scare the crap out of me."

Ryleigh wasn't sure whether to be flattered or cry at the unexpected admission, but didn't say anything. She was too surprised to form a coherent sentence even if he hadn't ordered her to not speak.

"With you there was nowhere to hide. You really nailed me. Every time you threatened to get past my defenses, I disappeared into work." Nick met her gaze. "You know me better than anyone so you'll be able to spot a lie a mile away. You're the only woman who ever made me want to lose control. Technically you have to have it before you can lose it. I was in over my head the first time I saw you and have been fighting that feeling ever since. I can't fight it anymore. If you give me a chance, I swear I'll never let you down again. I love that you love me. And I'm so damn tired of living half a life." He curved his fingers around her upper arms and tugged her close. "I love you. I want to marry you again. I want children with you."

Cautious hope turned into sheer joy as she recognized the intensity on his face for the sincerity it was. She did know him and he was telling the truth.

He waited for several moments and the intensity sharpened. "It would be good if you said something."

The happy news was dammed up inside her, and she couldn't wait to tell him. "I have permission to speak?"

"As if you need it." One corner of his mouth curved up. "Permission granted. What are you thinking?"

"It's really good you want to marry me for two reasons. Number one: I love you, but you already know that."

There was relief along with a smile in his eyes. "What's the second reason?"

"I'm pregnant."

"But—" Nick stared hard at her, then dragged his fingers through his hair. "I thought we missed the fertile window."

"Apparently the email and internet elves were wrong. I just did the test. Come and check it out for yourself." She took his hand and pulled him into the bathroom to look. "See?"

He stared at the stick. "The plus sign means you're—"

"Pregnant. That's why I've been so tired."

Ryleigh recognized the emotion on his face because she'd just experienced it herself. He went from stunned shock to unconcealed joy. It was beyond wonderful to see his awed reaction and share the excitement with him.

"My boys are badass," he said proudly.

She grinned. "What about my eggs?"

"Superior. Awesome." Then he turned serious. "I'm going to be a father."

"I'm going to be a mother. Finally." She snuggled her cheek on his chest. "And the best part is this baby doesn't exist because we made a bargain. He or she was conceived because we love each other."

"That's the headline. *Love trumps science and technology.* And isn't it lucky that I came over here with the intention of making an honest woman of you."

"You're the only man I've ever wanted to make me an honest woman."

She'd come to him because she wanted a child and was prepared to do anything except fall in love. But love was all she needed to have the doctor's baby.

* * * * *

Harlequin®

COMING NEXT MONTH

Available July 26, 2011

SPECIAL EDITION®

REQUEST YOUR FREE BOOKS!

2 FREE NOVELS PLUS 2 FREE GIFTS!

♦ Harlequin®

SPECIAL EDITION

Life, Love & Family

YES! Please send me 2 FREE Harlequin® Special Edition novels and my 2 FREE gifts (gifts are worth about $10). After receiving them, if I don't wish to receive any more books, I can return the shipping statement marked "cancel." If I don't cancel, I will receive 6 brand-new novels every month and be billed just $4.49 per book in the U.S. or $5.24 per book in Canada. That's a saving of at least 14% off the cover price! It's quite a bargain! Shipping and handling is just 50¢ per book in the U.S. and 75¢ per book in Canada.* I understand that accepting the 2 free books and gifts places me under no obligation to buy anything. I can always return a shipment and cancel at any time. Even if I never buy another book, the two free books and gifts are mine to keep forever.

235/335 HDN FEGF

Name	(PLEASE PRINT)

Address	Apt. #

City	State/Prov.	Zip/Postal Code

Signature (if under 18, a parent or guardian must sign)

Mail to the **Reader Service:**
IN U.S.A.: P.O. Box 1867, Buffalo, NY 14240-1867
IN CANADA: P.O. Box 609, Fort Erie, Ontario L2A 5X3

Not valid for current subscribers to Harlequin Special Edition books.

Want to try two free books from another line?
Call 1-800-873-8635 or visit www.ReaderService.com.

* Terms and prices subject to change without notice. Prices do not include applicable taxes. Sales tax applicable in N.Y. Canadian residents will be charged applicable taxes. Offer not valid in Quebec. This offer is limited to one order per household. All orders subject to credit approval. Credit or debit balances in a customer's account(s) may be offset by any other outstanding balance owed by or to the customer. Please allow 4 to 6 weeks for delivery. Offer available while quantities last.

Your Privacy—The Reader Service is committed to protecting your privacy. Our Privacy Policy is available online at www.ReaderService.com or upon request from the Reader Service.

We make a portion of our mailing list available to reputable third parties that offer products we believe may interest you. If you prefer that we not exchange your name with third parties, or if you wish to clarify or modify your communication preferences, please visit us at www.ReaderService.com/consumerschoice or write to us at Reader Service Preference Service, P.O. Box 9062, Buffalo, NY 14269. Include your complete name and address.

HSE11B

*Once bitten, twice shy. That's Gabby Wade's motto—
especially when it comes to Adamson men.
And the moment she meets Jon Adamson her theory
is confirmed. But with each encounter a little something
sparks between them, making her wonder if she's been
too hasty to dismiss this one!*

*Enjoy this sneak peek from ONE GOOD REASON
by Sarah Mayberry, available August 2011
from Harlequin® Supperromance®.*

Gabby Wade's heartbeat thumped in her ears as she marched
to her office. She wanted to pretend it was because of her
brisk pace returning from the file room, but she wasn't that
good a liar.

Her heart was beating like a tom-tom because Jon Adamson had touched her. In a very male, very possessive way.
She could still feel the heat of his big hand burning through
the seat of her khakis as he'd steadied her on the ladder.

It had taken every ounce of self-control to tell him to
unhand her. What she'd really wanted was to grab him by
his shirt and, well, explore all those urges his touch had
instantly brought to life.

While she might not like him, she was wise enough to
understand that it wasn't always about liking the other person. Sometimes it was about pure animal attraction.

Refusing to think about it, she turned to work. When
she'd typed in the wrong figures three times, Gabby admitted she was too tired and too distracted. Time to call it a
day.

As she was leaving, she spied Jon at his workbench in
the shop. His head was propped on his hand as he studied
blueprints. It wasn't until she got closer that she saw his

eyes were shut.

He looked oddly boyish. There was something innocent and unguarded in his expression. She felt a weakening in her resistance to him.

"Jon." She put her hand on his shoulder, intending to shake him awake. Instead, it rested there like a caress.

His eyes snapped open.

"You were asleep."

"No, I was, uh, visualizing something on this design." He gestured to the blueprint in front of him then rubbed his eyes.

That gesture dealt a bigger blow to her resistance. She realized it wasn't only animal attraction pulling them together. She took a step backward as if to get away from the knowledge.

She cleared her throat. "I'm heading off now."

He gave her a smile, and she could see his exhaustion.

"Yeah, I should, too." He stood and stretched. The hem of his T-shirt rose as he arched his back and she caught a flash of hard male belly. She looked away, but it was too late. Her mind had committed the image to permanent memory.

And suddenly she knew, for good or bad, she'd never look at Jon the same way again.

Find out what happens next in ONE GOOD REASON, available August 2011 from Harlequin® Superromance®!

Celebrating

Blaze 10 *years of*
red-hot reads

Featuring a special August author lineup of
six fan-favorite authors who have written
for Blaze™ from the beginning!

The Original Sexy Six:

Vicki Lewis Thompson
Tori Carrington
Kimberly Raye
Debbi Rawlins
Julie Leto
Jo Leigh

Pick up all six Blaze™
Special Collectors' Edition titles!

August 2011

Plus visit
HarlequinInsideRomance.com
and click on the Series Excitement Tab
for exclusive Blaze™ 10th Anniversary content!

SPECIAL EDITION

Life, Love, Family and Top Authors!

IN AUGUST, HARLEQUIN SPECIAL EDITION FEATURES
USA TODAY BESTSELLING AUTHORS
MARIE FERRARELLA AND *ALLISON LEIGH*.

THE BABY WORE A BADGE
BY *MARIE FERRARELLA*

The second title in the **Montana Mavericks:
The Texans Are Coming!** miniseries....

Suddenly single father Jake Castro has his hands full with
the baby he never expected—and with a beautiful young
woman too wise for her years.

COURTNEY'S BABY PLAN
BY *ALLISON LEIGH*

The third title in the **Return to the Double C** miniseries....

Tired of waiting for Mr. Right, nurse Courtney Clay takes
matters into her own hands to create the family she's
always wanted— but her surly patient may just be
the Mr. Right she's been searching for all along.

**Look for these titles and others in August 2011
from Harlequin Special Edition wherever books are sold.**

BIG SKY BRIDE, BE MINE! *(Northridge Nuptials)* by *VICTORIA PADE*
THE MOMMY MIRACLE by *LILIAN DARCY*
THE MOGUL'S MAYBE MARRIAGE by *MINDY KLASKY*
LIAM'S PERFECT WOMAN by *BETH KERY*
